THROTTLED

A RYLIE COOPER MYSTERY

STELLA BIXBY

FERRY TAIL PUBLISHING LLC

This novel is a work of fiction. Names, characters, places, and incidents
are either a product of the author's imagination or are used fictitiously.
Any resemblance to actual persons, living or dead, businesses, events, or
locales is entirely coincidental.

Copyright © 2019 by Crystal S. Ferry

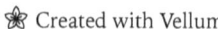 Created with Vellum

For My Amazing Husband
I love doing life with you. Thank you for all your support.

Two thousand dollars.

Two thousand dollars *per month*.

How could an apartment where I could cook an egg on the stove while simultaneously taking my morning poo cost two thousand dollars a month?

I prided myself on being a multi-tasker, but that was *so* not happening.

"What do you think dear?" The property management lady raised her white caterpillar eyebrows.

"*I* think it's lovely," my mother said beside me. She'd set up this whole meeting when I mentioned I'd finally saved enough to move out of her basement—or at least I thought I'd saved enough. Somehow Mom and this woman knew each other. Possibly through friends or a book club or, perhaps, Meddlers Anonymous. "Don't you think it's lovely, Rylie?" she asked as if she couldn't see my jaw hanging open.

"It's—um—small but . . ." lovely definitely wasn't the word. The exposed brick was pretty cool, but I suspected that was more a feature of disrepair than a stylistic choice. "Does the two thousand a month include utilities or a garage?"

"Goodness no." The woman laughed, and my mother laughed with her as if I'd said the funniest thing in the entire world. "All utilities are the responsibility of the tenant," she croaked, "and where you parked is the lot for the building. It was empty today because most people are at work, but it's first come, first serve with an additional $150 monthly parking pass."

My head spun. It wasn't as if I was trying to rent a fancy downtown Denver apartment. This was borderline bad side of town. And it would still cost more than half of what I made every month.

"I'm sorry, I don't think I can afford—"

"This is the cheapest unit in the metro area," she said matter-of-factly.

Mom had to have put her up to this. I gave her a sideways glance, but she was off inspecting the tiny toilet in the corner of the room. There was no way this-this . . . *room* was worth more than two thousand dollars a month. Well, other than for the fact it would get me out of my parents' basement.

Even so . . . I shook my head.

I couldn't do it. I wouldn't have money left to eat, let alone feed my dog, Fizzy.

"Thank you for showing me the place. I'll . . . think about it." As in, I'd be lucky to afford a cardboard box on the curb out front.

The woman's deeply creased face remained unchanged. "Are you sure? This one will be gone by tomorrow."

"I'm sure."

Gone by tomorrow? I wanted to meet the person who would shell out the kind of money to live in what felt more like a prison cell than a home.

I shook her wrinkled hand and Mom hugged her. "Thank you so much for meeting with us. Let me know if you find anything less expensive." I could have sworn Mom gave her a sly wink.

The parking lot was completely covered in slush from the previous night's snowfall and subsequent sunshine of this morning. A hundred and fifty bucks and they didn't even hire someone to plow? I'd be lucky if Cherry Anne, my Mustang, got out without getting stuck.

I turned the ignition over, and my heart raced with the power rumbling beneath me. The sound of 435 horses begging to be released never got old.

My mom sat in the passenger seat unusually quiet.

"What?" I finally asked.

"I feel *terrible* that you haven't been able to find an affordable place to rent."

Sure she did. "I'm sure I'll find something soon."

"You know, maybe you should wait." She looked straight ahead when she talked. "I have a feeling Garrett is going to propose soon, and you wouldn't want to be locked into a lease when you get married."

"I highly doubt I'll get engaged and married in the matter of a year." Just the thought seemed incomprehensible. "Plus, Garrett and I have only been dating a couple months. We're nowhere near getting married."

Mom quirked an eyebrow up at me.

"What? We're not."

"I see how he looks at you. And he's pretty wonderful."

She had conveniently forgotten about when she'd absolutely forbidden me from seeing him. I guess he *had* been a suspected murderer, but still, I knew he was innocent.

"One step at a time." I put the car in gear and inched forward so as not to dig my rear tires further into the slush only to spin out on the ice below.

"Just don't let him get away like you did with Luke."

"Luke chose to go in a different direction. I didn't let him get away." In fact, I'd practically thrown myself at him just to have him say we needed space so he wouldn't be my rebound. Now he was dating one of my co-workers.

"If you'd done more maybe . . ."

This conversation was going nowhere. "How's Megan?"

"She's been training for her ultra run thing."

Megan, my older sister, has the most energy of anyone I've ever known. Not only does she run marathons and triathlons, she also has four rambunctious little boys to keep her busy.

"How has work been now that you got the full-time position?" she asked. "I feel like I never see you anymore."

"It's been good," I said ignoring the passive aggressive comment. "Not that much different."

"Same job, better pay. That's great," Mom said. "And if you could just get away from homicides, it would be perfect."

As much as I wanted to roll my eyes, she was right. I

never thought being a park ranger would mean seeing so many dead bodies.

"I get my bulletproof vest soon." The moment the words escaped my lips, I wanted to shove them back in.

Mom's face turned a sickly grey almost as if she were about to pass out.

"It's just a precaution. None of the rangers have been shot at." I pulled into the driveway of my parents' upscale two-story house, and my mom got out of the car before I could even put it in park.

She slammed Cherry Anne's door so hard, it rattled my seat.

I should have known better than to bring up the safety aspect of the job. Mom had always thought being a ranger was too dangerous for me.

I followed her inside and was instantly greeted by Fizzy. "Hey, buddy." I scratched behind his ears.

"Hi, kiddo. What'd you do this time?" My dad joked from the comfort of his recliner.

"I mentioned my bulletproof vest," I replied sitting down on the couch next to his chair. He folded the paper and put it on the stand.

"You know your mother. Always worried about you and your sister."

I nodded. It wasn't as if her worries were completely unfounded. Less than a month into being a park ranger, I'd nearly been strangled to death by one of my co-workers. Then only a couple of months ago I'd been trapped in my boyfriend's basement by two murderous psychopaths —one of them Garrett's twin brother. I hadn't brought myself to tell Mom about the second incident though.

"I'm more careful now. I haven't encountered a murder in over two months. No dead people at all. Heck, I haven't had to take care of so much as a hangnail."

In all honesty, it had been a boring couple of months once summer had ended and the weather turned cold. People didn't spend much time at a reservoir when the water was too cold to boat on, and the ice was too unstable to do any ice fishing. They all went up to the mountains to ski and snowboard and snowshoe and snowmobile . . . my heart ached for those sports. I missed living in the mountains.

"Maybe I could take Mom snowboarding one of these weekends." I'd have to take a day off, but it would be fun. "And Megan could come too."

"I think that sounds like a wonderful idea," Dad said bringing out his proud smile. "When is the ice going to be strong enough for fishermen? I've thought about dusting off my old gear and trying my hand at catching some trout."

"I don't know. We've had some cold nights so I could see it being any time now."

Dad used to take Megan and me ice fishing when we were kids. Though we fished, our favorite part was riding the snowmobiles around on the ice. As a kid I never knew how dangerous it could be. Then I became a firefighter and had to go through ice rescue training.

"Maybe I could go with you sometime," I said.

"Sounds like a plan."

If I ever found an apartment that was even remotely affordable, I'd miss these moments.

2

"Ice rescue training," Greg—Ranger One—said as we stood at the edge of the ice waiting to be assigned a role. "Most of you have been through this, so it'll be a refresher. But we do have a first-timer." He smiled at Nikki with his grandfatherly smile—his salt and pepper mustache twitching upward.

Nikki looked stylish in her white ski pants and matching jacket. Her long auburn hair was pulled back into two French braids, and her makeup would probably stay absolutely perfect even getting in and out of the icy cold water.

No wonder Luke was dating her.

"Who would like to be the first victim?" Greg asked the group. Everyone hesitated.

"I can do it," I finally said.

"Great. Go ahead and put on the Gumby suit." He motioned to where we'd laid several billowing orange rubber suits over the hoods of our four-door Chevy ranger trucks. "And who wants to be the rescuer?"

Almost every hand shot up. Most of the guys wanted to be the hero. But Nikki stood off to the side looking like she might actually be nervous. I walked over to her once Greg had named Ben the rescuer and released us to get into position.

"You okay?" I asked.

"Of course I'm okay." Nikki bit back.

"It's okay to be scared. I was scared the first time I—"

"Shut it, Rylie. We all know you've done this before when you were a fancy firefighter." Every head turned at her outburst.

I put my hands up in surrender and walked away.

"What's the difference between a fancy firefighter and a regular one?" Seamus asked in his Irish brogue when I approached the trucks.

"Shut up," I muttered under my breath.

"I'm just jokin' with ya, blondie."

He and I had spent way too much time together the past two months. He was dating my best friend, Shayla, who had been a summer park ranger but was now finishing up police academy.

I pulled off my snow boots and stepped into the dry orange rubber suit. It was made to accommodate men much larger than my five-seven athletic frame making it billow out around me. Before putting my hands into the gloves, I pulled the hood over my head and down across my forehead, pushing the stray blonde hairs that hadn't fit in my ponytail up into the suit. Then I pulled on each sleeve as if I were pulling on a winter jacket only with gloves attached to the ends. My fingers were tiny

THROTTLED

compared to the massive gloves, but the wrist straps helped keep my hands from slipping out.

"Can you zip me up?" I asked Antonio who had just finished zipping up Ben's suit for him.

Antonio acted as if he hadn't heard me—I suppose maybe he actually hadn't—and walked away.

"I'll do it," Seamus said. He carefully zipped the suit up from my waist past my chin and over my mouth. "Looks like yeh won't be talking much." He laughed.

I pulled the suit down so I could still speak. "Yeah, fat chance."

"You ready?" Ben asked, his hulking frame nearly filling out the suit. For an older guy, he was in the best shape of all the rangers. Well, besides Dusty—he may have had Ben beat.

"Yep." I stepped gingerly through the snow and onto the ice where Antonio and Dusty had cut a hole earlier that morning.

The thrill of doing something I knew so well coursed through me. I may have been terrified the first time I'd had this training, but the minute I realized the suit made me practically invincible, my fears had been replaced with sheer excitement. Even when we'd been paged for ice rescue calls, there wasn't a sense of worry or dread because I knew we'd be able to get the person out of the water as long as they were still holding onto that ice shelf. My suit made me something of a superhero in my head and a giant floating bobber in reality.

I eased myself into the hole about fifty feet from shore. The air in the suit put me off balance until I tucked my legs up into my chest and curled into the tiniest ball I could make. A whoosh of air rushed out of my suit at the neck sucking the suit tighter to my body and giving me more control of my movement. Then I thrust my feet down toward the icy depths as hard as I could helping me to stay upright.

"Okay, Ben. Make sure you go through all the steps," Greg reminded him.

I pulled myself up to the ice shelf—the ice at least four inches thick—as Ben reached for my hand first. When that didn't work, he threw a rope to me.

"Don't grab it, Rylie," Greg instructed. "Pretend you're too cold."

I didn't do anything with the rope. Just let it skitter past my gloved hands.

"I'm going in," Ben notified the other rangers who held the rope attached to his suit at the waist.

Ben approached on hands and knees from the back of the hole, careful not to break the ice shelf I was holding onto. He eased himself into the water and curled into a ball like I had.

"Rylie, move your feet," Ben said. "Tuck them under the ice."

"They are tucked under the ice," I replied.

"Then what is below me?"

"What do you mean, what's below you?"

"I mean, there's something down there. And it's not a fish."

Instantly my mind went through all the possible scenarios.

Seaweed. Sunken boat. Dead body.

Oh God, please don't let it be a dead body.

"What's going on?" Greg asked. "Why aren't you rescuing her?"

Ben fumbled around behind me trying to pull whatever it was to the surface. I paddled my arms to slowly turn around.

"No, Rylie, you're supposed to stay on the ice shelf. What are you doing?" I had never heard Greg shout, but his voice was definitely more stern than usual.

I looked Ben in the eye, ignoring Greg. "What is it?"

Ben's face was red from the cold, but the look in his eyes was the same one I'd seen when we'd found a body stuck in a catfish trap over the summer.

"No," I said. "It can't be."

He pulled a bit harder and what looked like a human hand popped up to the surface.

I fought the urge to crawl out of the hole. There was not enough room for three of us in such a small piece of open water.

"I think we need some help over here," I yelled.

Greg walked up behind me and caught a glimpse of what had us completely distracted from the task at hand.

"Not another one," he murmured, his hand rubbing his forehead.

3

While Ben and Greg worked on hauling the body out of the water, I pulled myself up onto the ice shelf and rolled away from the hole like we were taught in the self-rescue section of the training.

Greg yanked on the hand and Ben helped him lift the body onto the ice. The cold water had done nothing to preserve the person's features. It looked like a big blob of human flesh.

Ben pulled himself out of the water as Greg took a pulse. I guess it was standard operating procedure, but anyone could have seen this person had been dead for a while.

"Yeh did not seriously find another dead body?" Seamus asked.

I shrugged. Maybe being a park ranger wasn't for me. They'd found more dead bodies since I'd worked here than ever in the history of the ranger program.

"Someone should probably call the police," Greg said. "It looks like our training is over."

Nikki's face was the only one of joy. I almost felt bad for her. I knew how it felt to be afraid of ice rescue. But she didn't have to be such a jerk to anyone who tried to help her.

"Don't be so sure," Dusty said, his biceps bulging from under his white long-sleeved shirt that complemented his dark brown skin. "I don't think we're going to need the police."

"Just because the body is obviously cold and dead, doesn't mean we shouldn't call it in," Greg said.

"Look at it more closely."

We all turned and looked harder.

Then, one by one, we all began to chuckle then laugh then gasp for air.

It wasn't a dead body. It was the dummy the lifeguards lost over the summer.

Ben's face returned to normal, and Nikki's went back to a state of fear. Thank goodness I wouldn't have to deal with yet another dead body and subsequent murder investigation.

"Great job," Greg said as he handed us our official Ice Rescue Certificates. "Now everyone can respond to ice rescue calls as needed."

The training room was quiet with exhaustion. As the sun had risen, we'd each taken our turn as rescuer, victim, and rope puller. Nikki went last and busted through the training as if it were nothing. My sympathy for her fear flew away on the cool winter breeze as she self-rescued effortlessly, stomped over to the ranger trucks, and peeled off her suit declaring we could all go in now.

"Tomorrow we'll do snowmobile training—or a refresher for those of you who have already gone through the training."

Chairs scraped the floor as everyone prepared to leave.

"Nikki and Rylie, hold up a minute," Greg said.

Seamus shot me a questioning look, and I shrugged.

"What's up?" I asked.

"You two need to head out to the equipment store to get fitted for your vests." He tapped his chest where his bulletproof vest sat under his blue uniform shirt.

"Together?" Nikki spat.

"Yes, together," he replied in a tone similar to the one my father used when my sister and I fought over whose turn it was to do the dishes when we were kids.

"Ugh, fine," Nikki stomped toward the stairs leading down to the garage bays where the ranger trucks stayed when not in use. "I'm driving," she yelled over her shoulder.

I glanced again at Greg, and he gave me a sympathetic smile. "Don't forget to tell them Greg sent you and to charge it to the city. Can you also pick up the new shirts we ordered?"

"Sure thing," I said.

Nikki was already sitting in the driver seat of the huge black Chevy pickup when I jumped in. "Greg said we needed to pick up some shirts while we're up there too."

"Whatever," she said and practically squealed the tires

pulling out of the shop and onto the road leading out of the park.

At first, the silence was fine. I didn't care that she didn't want to talk to me. It wasn't as if I really wanted to talk to her either. But the death glares she shot me every two minutes got to me more quickly than I'd anticipated.

"What is your problem?" I blurted out.

"Like you don't know," she took a corner so sharply the back tire popped up onto a curb.

"You were afraid of ice rescue training. I get it. I was when I first did it too."

She slammed on the brakes at a red light and looked over at me with the death stare of a two-year-old who didn't want to take a bath. "Ice rescue? You think this is about ice rescue?"

I wracked my brain. What else could it be? "You're not still mad that Luke and I had a thing, like, forever ago are you?"

"Oh yeah, *forever* ago. I know you've been texting and talking on the phone early in the morning and late at night."

"Me? Texting Luke?" The last time I'd texted or called Luke was when I'd come across a severed head in the trunk of my car. And he hadn't answered so . . .

"Don't play dumb with me." She hit the accelerator and drag raced a granny in a town car next to us.

"You should really watch how you're driving in the ranger truck. Fishbowl and all." Greg constantly harped on how we were all in a fishbowl. People watched every move we made and would only be too happy to report us to upper management.

"Don't tell me how to drive. And stop denying you talk to Luke."

"I seriously don't talk to Luke. Ever. I'm with Garrett, you know that, right?"

"Yes. I know that. Luke talks about it all the time."

"Sounds like you should discuss this with him."

"I have. He denies it's you."

"That's because it's not me. Here," I shoved my phone into her face, "do you want to see my phone? You can check my text messages."

"You probably delete them."

"Why would I delete them?" This girl was freaking nuts.

"Because you don't want Garrett to find them. Maybe I should tell him about all of this."

"Go for it. He knows exactly where I am in the mornings and in the evenings and, trust me, it's not talking on the phone." Actually, it didn't include much talking at all.

I smiled to myself.

"Stop smiling. You're just covering for him." Tears began to form in her eyes.

"Nikki, I know we haven't exactly gotten along since we've met, but I would never date someone in a relationship, nor would I cheat on anyone. I've been cheated on and it sucks. I wouldn't want anyone else to go through that."

"But you and Antonio totally hooked up while he was still married."

If I had been driving, we would have crashed.

I jerked my head toward her so violently I thought my neck might snap. "I most certainly did not hook up with

Antonio. Not while he was married. Not since he's been divorced. Not ever." Now it was my turn to be mad. "Did he tell you we did?"

I knew they were close, but I didn't take him for one to make up stories. Especially about me to Nikki. Granted, he *had* been ignoring me a lot lately.

"He didn't have to." Her tone was smug. "Luke and I just knew." She pulled the truck into a parking spot and turned to look at me.

It was nice to know she and Luke had nothing better to do than sit around and speculate about whom I was sleeping with.

Fun.

"Maybe the two of you should get a life and get out of mine."

I opened the door and slammed it behind me leaving her in the truck. I didn't have time for her shit today.

I marched into the uniform store to find rows and rows of various pieces of equipment, boxes of boots, tactical gear, hats, gloves, guns, knives—basically everything you'd need if you were in law enforcement.

"I'm a Prairie City Ranger. I'm here to get fitted for my bulletproof vest."

The lady behind the counter reminded me of one of my friends in high school. Dyed black hair, tribal tattoos running the length of her arms, and piercings all over her face.

"You one of Greg's bunch?" she asked thumbing through the neat stack of papers in front of her.

"Yep."

"Says here there's supposed to be two of you."

"She's coming." I motioned to the door where Nikki walked in like she owned the place.

"Just head on back. Michelle will take care of you."

I thanked her and made my way through the tightly packed store to where she'd motioned.

Michelle was busy talking to a man at the gun case, so I decided to look around and avoid Nikki at all costs. My pulse was finally starting to even out.

"It's not in yet? I ordered it two months ago," the man yelled across the counter.

"I'm sorry, Officer Ward, we've had a bit of a mix-up. It'll be another week or two." Michelle's voice was overly sweet. "If this is your duty weapon, I'm sure the department can come up with a substitution for the time being?"

"It's a personal purchase."

Michelle seemed relieved as her mouth turned upward at the corners. "I'll be sure to call you myself the moment it arrives."

The man huffed away with a mumbled thanks.

I took the opportunity to introduce myself. "Are you Michelle?" I asked.

"Sure am." The woman smiled. "How can I help you?"

"I'm here to get fitted for my bulletproof vest."

I heard Nikki clear her throat behind me.

"We both are."

"Perfect. Let's head over here and get your measurements." Michelle was as tall as Nikki but with smooth dark skin and a head of silky black hair. She pulled out a flexible tape measure like my mother used when sewing and instructed me to lift my arms. After taking what seemed like more measurements than needed, she moved onto Nikki.

"Do you often get people like that guy?" I asked.

"What guy?" Nikki asked.

"He was a joy, huh?" Michelle laughed while jotting down Nikki's tiny waist measurement. "Nah, usually people are really nice. He's just pissed because he didn't get his gun on time. I'd probably be pissed too."

I nodded. Never once had I ever considered getting a gun, let alone getting so mad over one.

"All done ladies. Now just remember you can gain some weight—the straps will stretch some—but not too much without the vests having to be altered so don't get all fat like me." She laughed at herself and walked back to the gun counter. "I'll get these submitted. They should be here in about two weeks."

"That reminds me, we are supposed to be picking up a bunch of new uniform shirts," I said.

Nikki hung behind me, her arms crossed over her chest.

"For Greg?" Michelle smiled. "I really like Greg."

Everyone did. He was impossible to dislike.

While she disappeared into the back room, I eyed the guns in the case. The last time I'd held one was when I was with my ex, Troy. He'd taught me to shoot when we'd first gotten together.

"He's leaving, you know?" A whisper came from beside me making me nearly jump into the glass display.

"What?" I turned to see Nikki examining the rough edge of the glass case.

"He signed up to go to the Middle East to help train law enforcement units."

"Luke? Luke did this?" I asked. My head was spinning. Of course, I was with Garrett now, and Luke and I were ancient history, but I still didn't want him to leave the country.

"Yes. Luke did this." She looked up into my face. "You really didn't know, did you?"

"I told you, he and I don't talk."

"If he's not talking to you, who is he talking to?"

Why did I care? I didn't need to care. I hadn't seen Luke for years before we'd reconnected this past summer. It wasn't as if he and I were ever going to get together.

"Has he been accepted? Or did he just apply?"

"He said he applied."

"Then he might not even go, Nikki." Troy had applied once and had never been accepted. "I wouldn't get so worked up over it. Not yet, at least."

It hit me at that moment just how serious their relationship was. She wouldn't be freaking out if this were the fling I'd imagined in my mind. That fact soured my stomach and made me hate myself for reacting that way. It may be true that I'd never cheat physically on Garrett, but if my heart couldn't get over a certain someone, was it really being faithful to my actual boyfriend?

No.

I *was* over Luke. Definitely. I was only worried about his safety. If he went to the Middle East, he might never come back. And if he never came back . . .

"Thanks, Rylie," Nikki said quietly. "Sorry I accused you of going behind my back."

Was she really being nice to me?

I opened my mouth to speak when Michelle popped out from the back. "Here you go, ladies. These shirts will look nice on you."

The shirts looked downright heavenly. They were the cleanest, most wrinkle-free uniform shirts I'd ever seen. I wanted to hug them.

"Sign here that you received them," Michelle said, and Nikki signed on the line.

"Let's get back to the reservoir, my shift is almost over," Nikki said practically throwing the pen on the counter. "And don't bother trying to talk to me in the truck. We're not friends."

"Damn," Michelle whispered as we walked away.

4

Every part of my body ached with exhaustion. Though ice rescue was my favorite of the trainings, it still left me feeling like I'd run a marathon.

The sun formed a beautiful orange and blue sunset over the snowy prairie. I sipped my coffee while keeping warm in the ranger truck.

The park was nearly empty besides the couple of ice fishermen who seemed to be making their way off the ice and three high-school kids messing around on the beach. The kids weren't dressed for the weather. The girl with long blonde hair wore black leggings, a white shirt that covered her butt, and a crop leather jacket. The two boys wore jeans and hoodies—each with the local high school football logo.

It was apparent the taller boy with dreamy brown hair was dating the girl, and the shorter boy with dirty blond hair was completely jealous. The couple would hold hands and kiss and playfully push each other toward the ice while the third sulked behind, flashing a smile anytime the other two looked at him. Typical high school drama.

A tap on my window nearly made me spill my coffee all over my button-down uniform shirt.

"Sorry, Rylie, didn't mean to scare you," Reginald, one of the daily ice fishermen said when I rolled down the window.

"It's okay. I was off in my own world."

"Young love. Sweet." He nodded towards the kids who were now testing the strength of the ice near the shore. "Maybe not terribly smart though." Polly—his tiny white dog—popped her head out of the collar of his jacket.

I laughed. "How was the fishing?" I should have checked his fishing license, but I'd already seen it about a hundred times since the reservoir froze over. I knew he was legit.

"It was okay. I think your training session scared all the fish away." He scratched Polly behind the ears, and she licked his nose.

"Sorry about that," I said. "Just making sure we can save you if you get in a bind."

Reginald—probably in his mid-seventies—looked like he could be Beyoncé's grandfather. He even had the same hair. "In that case, I guess I'll give you a pass." He winked, not in the creepy way some of the fishermen did, but in the cute old man way.

"Have a good evening," I said as he walked back to his truck. "Bye Polly."

"You too," he called out over his shoulder.

I watched the kids as long as I could before I had to begin my closing routine. Being that the park wasn't busy

23

in the winter months, there usually was only one ranger at Alder Ridge Reservoir to close. And since the sun went down so early, we closed earlier too. That only meant that I'd be back first thing the next morning to open again.

After closing the smaller gates on the back side of the reservoir, I returned to the plaza and closed up all of the bathrooms and offices.

The only car left in the lot belonged to the teenagers, and they zoomed past my truck on my way to check on them. Everyone was so afraid of getting a ticket for being in the park too late—or maybe they thought I'd lock them in and then their parents would freak out. Either way, I was only too happy to put the truck in the shop and take off in Cherry Anne. I popped the trunk to put my bag in and nearly fell backward.

There was a body. In my trunk. The same place where a severed head had lived for over a week this past fall.

"Ranger Seven, Ranger Two." My hands shook as I clicked the mic. "I'm going to need some assistance at the shop." Seamus was working a trail shift that evening.

"I'll call yeh on yer cell," he said.

"I need to call the police," I managed to squeak out. Before he responded, my cell rang in my pocket. "I found another body," I said when I answered. "I need to call the police."

"Can yeh describe the body for me?" Seamus asked.

I didn't want to describe the body. I didn't want to be anywhere near the body.

"I'm just going to call the police, and they can take care of it, okay?" I started to hang up, but Seamus called out.

"Hold on, don't hang up Blondie."

"What?" I hissed into the phone.

Why were dead bodies always finding me? Why Cherry Anne?

"It's not a dead body. Don't call the police," I heard footsteps coming from around the side of the building. I instinctively grabbed for my pepper spray.

"Whoa, whoa! Put it down," Seamus said.

The one light that cast an eerie glow on the parking lot in front of the shop revealed Seamus walking toward me.

"What are you doing here?" I hung up my phone and shoved it back into my pocket.

The smile on his face made me want to punch him.

"Yeh look like shit, Blondie." He sauntered over to the back of my car. "Like yeh seen a ghost."

"Just a dead guy." How was he this nonchalant? "Can I please call the police now?"

"I think yeh need to take a better look."

I begrudgingly walked to where Seamus stood next to my work bag that I'd dropped in the snow. At first, I felt like my insides might revolt, but then I realized what was really in my trunk.

My heart rate was through the roof. I turned and punched Seamus in the arm.

He didn't even miss a beat before laughing so loudly it could have cracked the ice.

"You are such a jerk." I yanked the dummy from the trunk of my car and tossed it into the snow. It was a wonder Shayla liked this man.

"Yeh. Should. Have. Seen. The. Look. On. Yer. Face," he said between gasps of air.

I tossed my work bag into the trunk. "Are you going to leave or should I lock you in?"

He grabbed his keys from his belt. "Yeh can't lock me in if I have keys to get out."

"Whatever," I opened Cherry Anne's door and slid inside. "I have to be back to open in the morning. I'm going home."

"Come on. It was a little funny, yeah?"

I couldn't help but smile. "Maybe a little."

"Can yeh imagine if yeh'd found a body in your trunk? I think yeh might've gotten fired just for stirring up so much shit since yeh've been here."

He was probably right. Four murders since I'd been hired. One more and I could be terminated for sheer superstition.

5

The morning came too early. Getting home after my parents went to bed and leaving before they woke up had its benefits, as did having two entire days off after working such long shifts.

I opened the gates and headed to the office to check the phone messages. Seamus hadn't followed me out the night before, claiming he needed to do paperwork, so I was on guard. I wasn't going to let him get to me again. My eyes were peeled for a dummy sighting.

After turning off the alarm systems, I unlocked the same bathrooms and offices I'd locked the evening before and headed to the ranger office with my huge latte. The light on the phone was lit up indicating there was at least one message.

I punched in the numbers to access the messages and pulled out my pen and notepad from the pocket on my shirt.

"You have three new messages," the message lady's voice said. "Message one, five forty-five PM."

"Hey there Rangers. This is Michelle over at Hentemens Supply. I wanted to let you know the vests will be here more quickly than we thought. Probably by next week. I'll let you know for sure. See you later. Buh-bye."

A smile breached my face. Was it weird I couldn't wait to get my vest?

"Message two, five fifty-two AM."

"Uh, hey Greg," a man's voice started. "It's Dave . . . the fisherman." Ah, Dave. The one I'd helped get out of prison. "I wanted you to know I saw some weird lights in the reservoir tonight. I wasn't in there or anything. I wouldn't do that . . . again. Promise. I was just driving by and saw. Maybe flashlights or something. Probably just kids being kids. But, uh, thought you should know."

Sure he wasn't in the park. I very clearly remember him being taken away in cuffs because he had been in the park after hours trying to catch that big catfish.

Damn fishermen.

I jotted down a note to pass onto Greg later that day.

"Message three, six twenty-two AM."

I looked at my watch. Six thirty. This one had just come in.

The sound of sobs echoed from the speaker through the office. It went on for about fifteen seconds before the line disconnected. I played the message over and over again. The second and third time hearing some traffic in the background and maybe a barking dog. But otherwise, there was nothing there.

For a moment I sat in silence staring at my notes.

- *Female? Sobs*

- *Traffic in background*
- *Dogs barking?*

I saved the message to play for one of the guys when they got in later and shoved my notepad back into my pocket. Something didn't seem right, but there was nothing I could glean from a few seconds of sobbing on an answering machine. Maybe it was a wrong number.

Hopefully.

I locked the office back up but didn't set the alarm so Carmen didn't have to worry about disarming it when she got in a couple of hours later. My truck had already lost all of the heat I'd accumulated driving around opening the gates that morning. The wind whipped the freshly fallen snow around making sparkly little tornadoes in the rising sunlight.

The truck tires crunched through the snow on the road that hadn't yet been plowed by the maintenance crew as I made my way to the parking lot where the ice fishermen parked. Three trucks sat in the lot, and three little tents dotted the ice out past the hole we'd coned off from yesterday's ice rescue training.

My coffee was running low—the fresh pot I'd made at the shop called my name. I put the truck in gear until I saw something—or was it someone—lying in the snow on the beach. I returned the truck to park and left it running as I jumped out.

Seamus wasn't going to fool me again. It was clearly

the dummy. Putting it in my trunk had been one thing, but out in the middle of the beach? I was surprised I hadn't gotten any calls about it from the fishermen.

As I approached, though, it was apparent that the fishermen used a different path to get out on the lake than the one leading to the dummy.

A dusting of snow covered the silicone form and the completely undisturbed area around it. I grabbed for one of the arms with my gloved hand and began dragging it back to the truck.

Apparently, these things were porous because it was heavier than I expected. Or maybe it was just frozen to the ground.

Dammit, Seamus. I couldn't just leave it there.

I used both hands this time and pulled with all my might until it groaned.

I released the arm falling back on my ass into the wet snow.

No.

It couldn't have groaned.

It was just my imagination. Or Seamus had added sound effects.

A chill formed at the back of my neck. I stood and brushed myself off.

The body—er dummy—was still covered in a thin layer of snow but as I looked closer, I could see what I hadn't before. Dirty blond hair frozen to the ground as if it had been gelled like that.

The dummy didn't have hair.

6

I yanked off my glove and pushed my fingers to the side of the guy's neck. It was weak, but it was there.

A pulse.

"Oh thank God," I said aloud before turning my radio over to dispatch and calling for help.

The ambulance crew was on scene within minutes and Luke and his partner, Jerry, arrived right behind them.

The paramedics jumped out of the ambulance and began rushing around trying to get the guy covered and on a backboard as gently as possible.

"The less we have to move him, the better his chance of survival." One of the paramedics said. "How long has he been out here?" He asked me.

I looked closer at the man—or rather, teenage boy. He was naked besides his pink heart boxers. "I'm not sure. It hasn't snowed since I opened the gates, but the wind has been pretty brutal so it could have covered him."

The paramedic nodded, "Good job keeping him covered with the snow. Instincts may tell you to brush it away, but it actually acts as an insulator. It may have been what kept this guy alive." They began to load him very gently into the back of the ambulance. "Turn the heat down. We can't warm him too quickly," the paramedic told the two others. "We'll just have to wear our jackets on the way to the hospital."

"How do you know so much about hypothermia?" I asked.

"I grew up in Alaska. People were always getting it some way or another." He winked and jumped in the back.

"Do you know him?" Luke asked suddenly at my side.

"Nope," I replied. "But he seemed nice." I shrugged. "I didn't expect you to show up when I called this in."

Luke looked down at his leather boots already wet from snow. "We were in the area."

I thought I heard Jerry scoff behind me.

"Well, I guess you can go now," I said. "Since, for once, I didn't find a dead person."

"This is a crime scene until we can determine it was an accident," Luke said. "Guys don't usually just lie down on an icy beach half-naked and allow themselves to freeze almost to death."

"Maybe he was suicidal?" I asked.

Jerry piped in, "I've never heard of someone killing themselves with hypothermia. I'm bettin' he did it for a girl."

A girl. My mind rushed back to the message on the answering machine. Could they be related?

"Um, I'm not sure if this has anything to do with, well, anything. But I got a weird message on the ranger line this morning."

"Wouldn't hurt to hear it," Luke said. "Jerry, do you mind securing the scene while I go with Rylie?"

Jerry murmured agreement along with the phrases "freezing my balls off" and "alone time."

I rolled my eyes.

"I can drive you over. It's too cold to walk." My nose and cheeks were chapped from the wind and bitter cold. I couldn't feel my toes even though I was wearing sub-zero socks and winter boots.

"Deal," Luke said jumping into the passenger side of the truck that was warm from running all this time. "It's nice in here."

I nodded. "I hear you signed up to go to the Middle East."

"You did, did you?" Luke chuckled.

"It's not funny. What's the deal?"

"I'm guessing Nikki told you?"

"She's really worked up over it."

"I didn't know you and Nikki were such good friends," Luke said with a half smile.

"We're not. She hates me. Actually, she thought you and I had been texting and calling at all hours of the day." I turned toward the office. "Who *are* you texting and calling all hours of the day if it's not me?"

"Whoa there. Slow down." Luke held his hands up as if motioning me to stop. "Nikki doesn't hate you—I don't think—she just gets jealous sometimes."

"She has nothing to be jea—"

"I know," Luke interrupted, "but she hasn't gotten over our history. As far as who I'm texting and calling, if she wanted to know, she could ask."

He left it at that. I opened my mouth to ask but then realized it really wasn't my business.

I could see him smiling from the corner of my eye.

"If you want to know, just ask," he said.

"It's none of my business who you are and aren't calling." I pulled into the ranger parking area and turned the truck off. "Just be honest with Nikki. Don't be the guy that makes a girl insecure just to have the upper hand."

Luke stepped out of the truck and followed me to the office.

"You know I'm not that kind of guy."

"I know," I said over my shoulder. "At least I don't think you want to be that guy. But sometimes it can feel nice to have a slight advantage in relationships. It makes us do things we shouldn't."

I thought about Garrett and me. Did either of us have the upper hand?

"Hey Rylie and—" Carmen—the big-boobed, big-haired, big-hearted secretary—almost spit out her coffee when she saw Luke walk into the office behind me. "Luke. What's going on? I saw the ambulance and police car. You didn't find another body did you?"

"Not a dead one," I said.

Carmen let out a snort like I'd just said the funniest thing in the entire world.

"We'll be in the office," I said.

She raised her eyebrows questioningly. I shook my head.

"Nice seeing you, Carmen," Luke said.

"Likewise," Carmen said.

Once we were in the office, I pulled the door closed so

we could listen to the message in peace. Which probably just added fuel to Carmen's skepticism fire.

"Like I said, I don't know if this has anything to do with the body, but I thought it was strange when I heard the message."

I fast-forwarded through the first message from Michelle and almost passed the second from Dave but then stopped. "Actually, this one might be important too." Duh, of course it would be. Dave saw people in the reservoir overnight.

"It's time stamped five fifty-two, meaning this kid was probably out here for a few hours," Luke said. "How did he survive?"

"Maybe he was messing around keeping warm for a while?" I threw out. "Why would he be out here in the freezing cold anyway?"

"Remember all the stupid things we did when we were teenagers?"

How could I forget? "Like the time we went sledding down the ski hill on a couch?" I offered.

"Or jumped into Big Lake with our prom clothes on?" Luke said. "Maybe this is something like that."

"It's a wonder we made it to adulthood alive."

Luke smiled the melty smile, and I looked away. I didn't need to have feelings resurfacing.

"Okay. Play the other message," Luke said.

I pushed the button, and we both listened to the girl sobbing.

"I know, it's just crying, but—"

"It might be something." Luke shrugged. "Or it might be nothing. We can always get the team on it to see where the call came from. At least a number from where she called. But I think Jerry and I will need to talk to Dave."

"I'm sure he'll love seeing you guys again." I rolled my eyes.

"You're right. Maybe you should come with me. Dave seems to like you."

Only because I cleared his name and got him out of jail by nearly being killed by someone other than Dave.

"Okay. I'll go with you," I said. "But I'll need to clear it with Greg first. Now that I'm a full-timer, I have more responsibilities."

"I know I congratulated you at the party, but we haven't really had an opportunity to talk. How is it going?"

"It's going really well. I didn't think I'd like being a park ranger as much as I do, but it's grown on me. The guys are great. Even Nikki is nice to me sometimes."

"So you feel like you're part of a team?" he asked leaning back in the office chair.

"I guess so. I mean, we are a team."

"Not like when you were a firefighter though?"

Was he a mind reader now?

"Not quite. Not yet." I stopped. "I don't know. Maybe that was just something I had because I was younger and had been there for so long. And it was volunteer. This is my job."

"I think you'll get there. It'll just take time and trust. Jerry might not be the model partner, but he and I are definitely a team. Shayla's mom and I were too. Give it a while."

"Speaking of Jerry," I said. "I bet he's done. Should we head back out?"

Luke nodded. We both stood at the same time creating an uncomfortable closeness of our bodies. It was funny, only a few months ago I would have used the proximity with Luke to my advantage, but now it just felt strange.

"Sorry." I laughed and tried to move out of his way. But he moved the same direction as we commenced the awkward shuffle. Finally, he put his hands on my shoulders.

"I'll go this way," he said. "And you—"

"What is going on here?" Nikki asked from the doorway.

We had been so caught up in our attempts at avoiding physical contact that we'd failed to realize we had an audience.

Luke's hands dropped to his sides, and I took the opportunity to sneak out the door., carefully moving past Nikki on my way.

"She sounded pissed," Carmen said when I got to the front of the offices.

"You could have given me a heads up," I whisper yelled.

"What was I supposed to do, let out a bird call?" Carmen shook her head. "She knew the two of you were back there anyway. Jerry musta told her. Did you at least kiss him?"

"Carmen! I have a boyfriend. He's with Nikki."

"Doesn't mean you two don't still spark."

"No. We did not kiss."

"Then what is she yelling about?"

Nikki was giving Luke an earful about being a cheater.

"I think it goes past today," I said. "And way past me."

"So Luke's cheating on her, huh?"

"No," I said too quickly. "I mean. I don't think Luke would do that."

"You know what, Nikki?" Luke's voice rose over Nikki's. "I'm not doing this anymore."

"What do you mean you're not doing this anymore?"

Now Carmen and I were both listening.

"I can't be with someone who constantly questions my character. I'm not that kind of guy. Everyone knows that. *You* should know that."

"So what? You're breaking up with me?" Nikki's voice was now laced with tears. "After all I've been through this morning?"

Carmen and I seemed to lean forward in unison. What was she talking about?

"What have you been through?" Luke asked, his voice tired and impatient.

"My cousin is missing, and his best friend is the one your *girlfriend* found on the beach."

Carmen sucked in a little gasp, and I covered her mouth with my hand.

"Alex?" Luke asked.

"Yes, Alex. I don't have any other cousins I'm close with," she was crying now. "And then I find you here in an embrace w-with—" the end of her sentence was muffled, likely because Luke had pulled her to his chest.

Carmen looked up at me, her eyebrows high on her forehead. I removed my hand. "We were not in an embrace," I whispered. "I'm going to go see how Jerry's doing."

I pulled my coat back on. It may have been past noon, but the sun was doing a poor job of warming anything.

———

Greg and Seamus stood with hot cups of coffee in their hands next to Jerry on the ice-covered beach.

"Hey Blondie," Seamus said handing me a Starbucks cup. "Thought yeh might need some extra caffeine today."

I wrapped my gloved hands around it greedily sipping the bitter, senses-jolting mix of coffee with too little cream. "Thank you." I smiled. "Did you find anything else?"

"No," Jerry said. "But it's the not finding anything that's a problem. Someone had to have taken this kid's clothes, or else he walked here naked. It looks like a prank gone wrong."

Jerry crossed his arms over his chest. "Any luck with the messages?"

"There was a message from Dave—yes, that Dave—saying he saw lights in the reservoir last night. And then there was an odd one that sounded like a girl crying."

"Does Luke think they're related?" Greg asked.

"He's not sure. I think the Dave one probably is. Luke said you two—" I turned to Jerry "—would go talk to him. And that they might be able to pull the phone records to find out where the crying girl called from."

"Maybe the kid'll wake up and tell yeh everything," Seamus offered.

"That would make my job a hell of a lot easier," Jerry said.

We all stopped talking as Nikki and Luke pulled up. Nikki's face was still red from crying.

"What's wrong with her?" Seamus asked while they were still out of earshot.

"The kid we found was her cousin's best friend," I whispered. "And her cousin has gone missing."

"Looks like we have a full day ahead of us," Jerry said.

Nikki and Luke approached, Luke keeping his gaze firmly on the ground.

"Nikki, why don't you take the day off?" Greg said.

"Don't we have snowmobile training this afternoon?" Nikki asked with a sniffle.

"Yeah, but you know how to drive a snowmobile, right?" Greg asked.

"I do," she said. "Yearly winter trips to Togwotee."

What the hell a Togwotee was, I didn't know, but it sounded expensive.

"We'll just go through the basics the next time you're on a trail shift," Greg said. "I'm really sorry you're going through all of this."

She thanked him, and Luke escorted her back to her truck.

"Do you think her cousin has something to do with this kid's accident?" Greg asked.

Jerry shrugged. "Can't ever tell. It would be helpful to find him, though."

"Ready?" Luke said when he returned alone.

Jerry nodded.

"See you later, guys," Luke threw up a wave, and we all said our goodbyes.

"Let's get up to the shop," Greg said. "The others will likely be up there ready for training."

Antonio, Ben, and Dusty huddled around the bed of Ben's truck bed in the shop bay when we arrived.

"It's about time you showed up," Ben said with a big smile.

"Rylie found another body," Greg said. "But it was alive," he added quickly.

"Where was Nikki going?" Dusty asked. "She tore out of here like a bat out of hell."

"Her cousin is missing, and it was his best friend we found incapacitated on the beach this morning," Greg answered. "She'll do her training another day."

Dusty shrugged his hulking shoulders.

"Let's get a move on," Greg said motioning toward the trailer with four snowmobiles on top.

7

The cold was enough to freeze you to the bone without driving thirty miles an hour on a roaring machine.

"Rylie, you have some experience with sleds—I mean—snowmobiles, right?" Greg asked in front of the group.

"I grew up on a snowmobile." I nodded.

"We're going to work in pairs," Greg said. "Seamus and Dusty, Ben and me, and—"

Ugh. Just say it.

"—Antonio and Rylie."

I snuck a glance to my right where Antonio stood with his arms crossed over his chest. He did not look happy.

"We'll start with loading and unloading the sleds on the trailer. Then we'll head out," Greg said. "We'll ride tandem into the field where we'll do the training."

Riding tandem.

With Antonio.

A shiver that had nothing to do with the cold ran down my spine.

Loading and unloading the sleds was so much easier with ramps to get them on and off. Unlike the tilt trailer I grew up with, these were stationary. It was just a matter of lining up the skis with the ramp.

"This area has been completely untouched," Greg said motioning to the opened gate that held a closed to the public sign. "The city acquired it late this fall and has yet to disclose the plans for its use."

The Prairie City property butted right up to the foothills of the Rocky Mountains, and I could picture Big Mountain—the town where I'd grown up—on the other side of the range. Dense patches of trees left barely enough room to get through on snowmobile. The meadows between the trees had to have several feet of snow, but these machines would be powerful enough to get through it without getting stuck.

"I'll lead the pack back to the clearing," Greg said getting on his snowmobile.

Antonio and I approached our sled at the exact same time.

"You can drive," we said in unison. I looked up at him and smiled thinking we could laugh at our slip, but he looked away, mounted the sled, and grabbed the handlebars.

I guess that meant he'd be driving. Fine with me.

It took me a minute to figure out where to put my hands. Normally I'd have held onto his waist, but with the weirdness surrounding us, I decided on the handles next to my hips. Hopefully, he didn't go too fast otherwise I'd probably fall off.

Greg and Ben led, and Antonio followed directly

behind. Antonio was stiff and non-moving with the machine. My assumption that he'd be more experienced on the snowmobile was apparently wrong.

We wove through trees and bushes three snowmobiles in a row until we reached a clearing. Antonio turned off the machine and slid off without so much as making contact with me. I kept my helmet on, only flipping up the visor, trying to retain any bit of warmth still left in my body.

The field in front of us was a snowmobiler's playground. Fluffy white snow covered what looked like logs and tree stumps several feet below the surface and maybe even a small frozen stream. More trees stood on the far side of the field and to each side were other fields just waiting to be disturbed by two skis, one track, and a whole lot of horsepower.

I could feel a smile spreading across my face.

This was exactly what I needed to get my mind off of all the craziness in my life. Some time when the only thing I could hear was the roar of the engine and the only thing I could feel was the vibration.

"There may be times we need to use the snowmobiles for rescues and the more land we acquire, the more possibility we'll be needed." Greg sat on the seat of his sled with his helmet resting in his lap. "Even though people aren't supposed to be back here, they always come whether on cross country skis, snowshoes, horses, or on foot. When there's a will, there's a way."

The thought of such pristine land being closed off to recreational use seemed wrong.

"Rylie, can you please point out some of the hazards

you might come across riding through this field?" Greg asked pulling me from my thoughts.

"It looks like there's a fallen tree over there," I pointed to where the snow heaved a bit. "And there could be a small stream with the slight trench in the snow there."

"Good observation," Greg said, an approving smile on his face. "As we make our way through this clearing, I want everyone to remember your body positioning on the sleds, potential obstacles, and the appropriate amount of throttle. This is not a speed course, but if you go too slowly, you'll end up stuck. Any questions?"

"Are we doing this tandem?" Antonio asked.

"No. We'll take turns."

"Good," Antonio murmured low enough he probably thought I couldn't hear.

I couldn't help but feel a pang of hurt by his constant dismissal. I thought we'd become friends when he helped me with the boat. He'd stood up for me and probably saved my job. He'd even flirted with me shamelessly.

But since I'd gotten the full-time position, he'd practically ignored me. Maybe it was all about the thrill of the chase with him. He flirted with the summies because he knew they'd be gone by the end of the summer.

I saw the behavior all the time growing up in a tourist town. People came and went, and there was always the promise to keep in touch, but it was an empty one. Some issued declarations of love at first sight only to never see one another again.

I'd had my fair share of summer and winter boyfriends. Ones who were gone before my heart could attach, but there long enough to enjoy. It was the epitome of non-commitment.

Antonio, Greg, and Dusty took the first turn through the meadow. Their joy was apparent as they tore through the powder dodging logs and stumps, jumping over mounds. I couldn't wait for my turn.

"Do you think Nikki's okay?" Ben asked Seamus and me.

"She seemed pretty shaken up," I said.

"She should be." Seamus brought his gloved hands to his mouth and blew hot air into them. "Her cousin is probably the prime suspect in this kid almost dying."

We stood in silence with our thoughts. I hadn't considered her cousin being a suspect. But it made perfect sense. He was missing, and his best friend had been left half-naked to die.

Eventually, the others returned and handed the snow-mobiles over to us.

I snapped the visor on my helmet down and slung a leg over the seat. When I pulled the cord, the engine revved to life sending vibrations through my body.

The field in front of me had practically been destroyed by the other guys so when Seamus and Ben took off in the path of the others, I veered to the left toward a more untouched area of snow.

Shifting my weight from one side to the other, I was able to control the way I maneuvered through the mounds of powder. Adrenaline coursed through me as I turned left and right sullying the smooth terrain.

But the terrain wasn't completely pristine. In fact, as I came to the top of a small ridge, it was a downright mess.

I made sure I wasn't in snow too deep before I let off the gas. The small meadow below looked like it had been the scene of a huge party.

I called over the radio to Greg.

"Ranger Seven, Ranger One."

"Go ahead," Greg said.

"Could you come over here and look at something with me?"

"I'm helping Seamus get his sled unstuck, Ranger Five could you assist Seven please?"

Why Antonio? Didn't Ben have the snowmobile?

"Copy," Antonio mumbled into the radio.

In less than five minutes Antonio pulled up next to me. "What's up?" he asked not looking at me.

"I could ask you the same." My frustration got the better of me and I no longer cared about the meadow. "What is your problem with me?"

"I do not have a problem with you."

"Then why won't you talk to me? Look at me? Did I piss you off somehow?"

"There is nothing wrong. Everything is the same as it has always been. Now, what did you need?"

My breaths came out in irritated puffs of air. I wanted to come back with every example of how things were not the same, but Antonio didn't look like he was in the mood.

"Look." I stepped aside so he could see the meadow behind me.

His eyes widened slightly. "Someone threw a party out here." He let out a long exhale. "Why do you always have to find shit like this?"

He wasn't joking. His tone was angry. "Ranger Five, Ranger One."

"Go ahead," Greg replied.

"Could you come over once you get Seamus out?"

"On my way."

Greg arrived momentarily. The three of us left our snowmobiles on the hill and walked down through the knee-deep snow to the meadow.

"It looks like someone had a rave out here," Greg said. "It is called a rave, right?"

"Party. Rave. Whatever it was, it looks like they had a good time," Antonio said picking up a red plastic cup.

A pit of charred wood still smoked a bit.

"They haven't been gone long," I said pointing to the smoldering wood. "How'd they get out here?"

Greg pointed to the south. "There's an access point just down from here. It wouldn't be hard to walk."

"Did you drive around this before we got here?" Antonio said, his voice accusing.

"No," I said. "I stayed up on the hill."

"Someone has been riding a snowmobile out here recently." He pointed to tracks leading away from the fire into the forest.

"They must not have gotten the snow or wind the reservoir did," Greg said. "The tracks are still pristine."

"Think we need to call PD?" I asked.

"Probably not," Greg said. "Take some photos, and I'll have Seamus set up a trail camera."

I pulled out my phone and started snapping photos of the area—cups that smelled of beer, snowmobile tracks, footprints, the fire. I had to have taken a hundred photos before we started the task of cleaning up.

Training ended with day old coffee, and a debrief at the shop. Antonio was still avoiding me, and everyone seemed tired from the past two days.

"Lively bunch we are, eh?" Seamus whispered to me.

I smiled. "Everything just feels weird."

"Like Antonio ignoring you?"

So he'd noticed too. "What's his problem?"

Seamus shrugged. "Beats me. What'd yeh do blondie?"

"I did nothing. He swears everything is fine."

"Yeah, okay."

Greg cleared his throat at the front of the room. "Good job today. We'll need to do more to patrol that area in the future."

Dusty and Seamus nodded.

My phone buzzed in my pocket. It was Nikki's number, of all people.

I need your help.

I read the message five times over.

"Everything okay?" Seamus whispered beside me.

I showed him the message—the only message I'd ever gotten from Nikki.

"If there's nothing else, we'll dismiss for the day," Greg said.

"Are yeh going to help her?" Seamus asked as we all stood and made our way down to where our cars were parked.

I shrugged. How could I not?

What do you need?

Meet me at North-Central Hospital.

"Just don't go getting into trouble," Seamus said reading the messages over my shoulder.

"Me? Trouble?" I laughed.

8

"Thanks for coming," Nikki said when I pulled into the parking lot next to her.

"What's going on?" I asked. Darkness had settled in for the night.

Nikki started walking toward the hospital entrance. "I need to find Alex. To clear his name."

"Maybe he doesn't want to be found," I said.

"Or maybe he's hurt somewhere," she said.

It was plausible. "How will being at the hospital find Alex? Do you think he is here, but no one knows who he is?"

Nikki looked at me like I was a complete idiot. "No."

The front doors made a whooshing sound when we walked through. The change in temperature was immediate with a burst of hot air coming from the ceiling.

I pulled my coat off.

"Luke said I should try to be friends with you rather than see you as an enemy." Nikki pulled off her scarf and hat, her hair perfect.

"That would probably be good," I said cautiously. It felt like a trap.

"So you'll help me?" she asked.

"Help you with what?"

"With finding Alex."

"Won't Luke?" I asked.

She waved a hand. "He's helping. He's being a cop. But he can't involve me. I'm a *civilian*." She said the word civilian as if it was a bitter word being spat out of her mouth.

"You've decided to go behind his back?"

"Don't look at me like that. You've done the exact same thing . . . twice."

She had me there. "Fine," I said. "But I don't want to step on Luke's toes."

She smirked. "You let me handle Luke."

From what it looked like back at the reservoir, she and Luke were on the outs, but I wasn't about to tell her that.

"Are you going to tell me what we're doing here?" I asked.

"This is where they brought Jordan—the kid you found." She started toward the elevator. "I wanted to see if he'd woken up."

Jordan's room was full of people when we arrived.

"Can I help you?" A small woman with bloodshot eyes met us at the door.

Nikki froze as if she didn't know what to say.

I stepped in front of her. "I'm Rylie. The park ranger

who found Jordan this morning. And this is Nikki—er—one of my co-workers." I didn't know if I should tell her that Nikki is Alex's cousin. We might get booted out.

The woman wrapped her arms around my torso and squeezed. "Thank you for saving my baby."

"You're welcome," I said. "How is he doing?"

She released me and looked over at Jordan who seemed so small in the hospital bed hooked up to monitors and tubes. "Not good," she said. "The doctor said he had alcohol in his system." She let out a sob. "And the alcohol may have made him think he was warmer than he really was. His body probably didn't show the normal signs of hypothermia and—" her voice cracked.

"I'm so sorry," I said.

She wrapped her arms around her body. "If you hadn't found him when you did, he'd probably be dead. At least he has a fighting chance now." Her smile was an attempt at positivity.

"Nikki?" A deep voice from the door made us turn. "What are you doing here?"

Nikki's face flushed. "I'm, um—" She looked at me.

"We're here to see Jordan," I said. "I'm Rylie." I held my hand out to the man who looked to be about our age and was handsome in a used-to-be-jock sort of way.

"Brody," he said. "I'm Jordan's football coach at North-Central High."

Nikki still didn't say anything.

"Rylie found Jordan this morning," Jordan's mother said.

"Ah," he said, his face darkening.

"Do you know why he might have had alcohol in his

bloodstream?" I asked surprising myself that I'd gone straight for the questioning.

Brody didn't look as taken aback as he should have. "We have a championship game coming up. We test for drugs before every game—school policy—but not alcohol."

He almost acted like it wasn't a big deal that one of his players had been drinking illegally.

"Is Jordan a starter?" I asked.

Jordan's mom turned her attention from Brody back to her son.

"No," Brody said slowly. "He's a good quarterback, but Alex Ward is the starter."

If Alex were the starter, he would have no reason to do something so terrible to Jordan. It would almost be the other way around.

"Have you found Alex yet?" he asked Nikki.

She shook her head and looked out the window.

Brody put an arm around her shoulder as if it was the most natural thing in the world. "They'll find him."

She leaned into him, and they stood there for a moment. Jordan's mother held Jordan's hand at his bedside. I tried to make sense of what was going on.

"Nikki?" Another voice—this one more familiar—came from behind me.

Nikki pushed away from Brody, but not before Luke had caught a full glimpse of them. He frowned but said nothing of it.

"I'm Luke," Luke said shaking Brody's hand in the tug-o-war kind of way guys did when they were trying to get the upper hand.

"Brody," Brody said.

Luke turned his attention on me. "What are you doing here?"

"Nikki and I wanted to check in and see how Jordan was doing." I tried to keep my voice as innocent as possible.

Luke wasn't buying it. "How is Jordan?" he asked.

"The same as this morning," his mom said. "They found alcohol in his bloodstream."

Luke nodded as if he understood how bad that could be. "I'd like to speak with you alone," he said to her. "If that's okay?"

Jordan's mom nodded and looked at us.

"We were just about to leave anyway," I said.

"Thank you for saving him," she said. "Even if he doesn't make it—" she choked on her words.

"He'll make it," Nikki said and turned to walk out the door. "He has to make it," she whispered to herself.

I followed behind, and Brody brought up the rear.

"I'm going to wait so I can see him," Brody said. "It was good seeing you, Nik."

Nikki smiled. "You too."

"What the hell was that?" I asked when we were out of earshot.

"What was what?" she said.

"You and Brody?"

She sighed. "Brody is my Luke."

"Huh?"

"He was my high school sweetheart. Like Luke was yours."

That explained a lot. "And now he's the high school football coach?"

"Best one they've had in years." She looked straight ahead when we entered the elevator.

"Don't you find it strange that he was completely unsurprised that one of his players had alcohol in his system?"

"High schoolers drink." She shrugged. "Didn't you?"

I lived in a town where everyone knew everything. My parents would have killed me. "Not really."

"Well aren't you just little miss perfect." Her sarcasm was biting.

"I'm trying to help. But if you'd like me to stop, I can."

"No. I'm sorry." We walked out of the elevator and into the lobby of the glass-walled building to find two teenage girls sitting on a couch whispering.

"What if they never find him?" The girl with curly black hair and dark complexion said.

"Maybe it would be for the better," the girl with long blonde hair and complexion so fair she would likely crisp in even the smallest amount of sun exposure replied.

"Debbie?" Nikki said and walked over to the blonde girl.

"Nikki," she said standing. A look of panic washed over her face. "Why are you here?"

"We just wanted to check to see how Jordan is. Rylie's the one who found him this morning."

It was hard to believe it had only been that morning since I'd found him lying on the beach.

"Wait, don't I know you from somewhere?" I asked the

girl. She looked oddly familiar. Then it hit me. "You were out at the reservoir last night, weren't you?"

She looked at her friend who shrugged a tiny bit.

"Yeah," she finally said.

"You were?" Nikki asked.

"Alex, Jordan, and I went out there before—"

Her friend elbowed her in the ribs.

"Before what?" I asked. "You know this could be critical to finding Alex."

Debbie didn't say anything.

"Don't you want to find Alex?" Nikki asked, her voice fragile.

"I guess, maybe." Debbie shrugged. "Or maybe not."

Nikki looked like she'd been slapped in the face.

"Why wouldn't you?" I asked.

"Look, Alex is an ass," Debbie's friend said. "He flat dumped Debbie last night in front of everyone."

"In front of everyone? Who's everyone?" I asked.

"The cheerleaders. The football players. Some of the other kids from school," her friend replied.

"The popular kids," I said.

"I guess so." She shrugged.

"Where was this meeting?" Nikki asked looking at Debbie.

"Out in the boonies," Debbie said even though her friend was shaking her head no. "And you want to know what I think about Alex's convenient disappearance? I think he tried to hurt Jordan and then took off. He's probably halfway to Canada with his new girlfriend by now."

"Why would he hurt Jordan?" I asked.

"Football, why else?" Debbie said.

"But Alex was the head quarterback. Jordan didn't have a chance at the position. Wouldn't it be the other way around?" Nikki asked.

"Alex was losing it." Debbie looked down at her nails. "He was skipping practices and going off alone a lot."

"With his new girlfriend?" I asked.

"How should I know?" Debbie said. "I thought everything was fine until last night."

It had looked fine when I'd seen them all together.

"So he broke up with you at this party in the boonies," I said. "And then what?"

"He left. Went home. Or to see his girlfriend. Or to plot Jordan's murder. How should I know?"

"Who is this girlfriend?" Nikki asked.

"Some loser, I'm sure," Debbie's friend said.

"A name would be helpful," I said.

"Trust me, if I knew who she was, she'd be in a world of hurt right now," Debbie said. "Come on." She grabbed her friend's hand and practically dragged her toward the elevators.

"Debbie sounds like a peach," I said when they disappeared behind the silver doors.

"She used to be so nice," Nikki said. "She even came to family functions. They'd been together for a really long time. I can't believe he broke up with her."

"Do you think maybe he was into something bad? I mean, if he was skipping practices—"

Nikki shook her head violently. "No way. He had a friend who died of a drug overdose his freshman year. He swore he'd never do anything more than a beer here and there."

"Something doesn't add up. I get why people would think Alex might have something to do with this incident with Jordan, but where did he go?" I said more to myself than to Nikki. "Maybe tomorrow we could casually go to football practice and find out if any other students have gone missing."

Nikki nodded. "Thank you for your help."

At this point, I wanted to know what was going on almost as badly as she did.

9

"I just can't believe you and Nikki are friends now," Shayla said after I told her about the day.

We met at Seamus's house to watch some movies since we all had the next day off.

"I don't know if I'd say we're friends." I took a sip of the Bud Light with lime and felt the cool bubbles washing my anxiety away.

"But she wants your help finding her cousin?" Shayla asked.

Garrett had his arm around me on one of Seamus's brown microfiber couches, and Seamus had his arm around Shayla on the other. Even though Shayla was nearly ten years younger than Seamus, they somehow fit together perfectly. Her innocence was magnified by his blunt Irish way.

"I think she wants to find him and clear his name. Almost everyone seems to think he was responsible for what happened to Jordan," I said, rubbing my thumb over Garrett's knee.

"What does Luke think?" Shayla asked.

I felt Garrett shift his weight beside me. He always got fidgety when Luke was mentioned.

"I don't know. He and Nikki got into a bit of an argument at the office today." I tried to leave all emotion out of my voice. Garrett deserved to feel as confident in our relationship as I did. "But the way she was acting, it was as if she didn't trust Luke to investigate properly."

"Most family members don't think the police do enough," Shayla said.

Her mom had been Luke's partner before she retired and Shayla herself was now nearing the end of police academy.

"What do *you* think, oh shit magnet?" Seamus asked.

I hesitated a minute. Neither my boyfriend nor best friend wanted to hear me say I'd be taking on another criminal case. "I don't know what to think. He broke up with his girlfriend at some sort of party last night after they looked pretty cozy at the reservoir yesterday afternoon."

"You saw them at the reservoir?" Shayla asked.

"All three of them," I said. "Jordan was definitely the jealous third wheel."

"But Alex broke up with her?" Garrett asked.

"That's what she said. She's convinced he has another girlfriend. That he's been acting weird."

"Maybe she killed him," Shayla said with a laugh. But the guys both looked at her with open mouths. "I'm kidding," she said. "Kind of."

I laughed. "I don't know that she killed him. At least I hope not." I thought about it for a minute. "She did seem pretty okay with the thought of him never being found, though."

"We don't need another murder investigation," Seamus said.

I snuggled a bit closer to Garrett, and he tightened his arm around me. "Agreed."

"Do they have any idea where Alex might have gone?" Shayla asked.

"Not that I know of," I said. "Nikki seems super scattered about the details."

"Probably doesn't help that she and Luke are on the outs," Seamus said.

"What?" Shayla asked sitting up so quickly her pretty blonde ringlets bounced with the motion.

"He signed up to go to the Middle East." I shrugged. "She's pretty pissed about it."

"Why would he go Middle East?" Garrett asked.

"To train people in other countries to be police officers," Shayla answered settling back in against Seamus. "It's a great way to make a whole bunch of cash if you're willing to leave everything and put your life on hold for a year or more. I know several officers who've done it. I guess it only makes sense for Luke to do it too."

Her expression showed the same feelings I had. We'd both had a thing for Luke at one point, and now we were both in happy relationships. That didn't mean we didn't care if he put himself in danger.

"Anyway, how's the apartment search going?" Shayla asked, changing the subject.

I laughed. "You should have seen the place my mom took me to the other day. It was teeny tiny and two thousand dollars a month, not including parking or utilities."

Shayla shook her head. "That's nuts."

"The guys and I pay three thousand here," Seamus said. "Thankfully there are three of us. I can't imagine trying to find a place by myself."

Garrett shifted next to me. "You could always move in with me," he said.

Shayla's big eyes widened. Seamus raised his eyebrows.

I didn't know what to say. Part of me *had* thought about it—the part that was falling for one of the nicest men I'd ever met. But then I remember how clean everything was at his place and how—well—not clean I am.

"Sorry, I didn't mean to put you on the spot," he squeezed my shoulders again. "Just a thought."

The room was silent. We all took long swigs of our beer.

"Looks like it's movie time," Seamus finally said.

"I'm really sorry for bringing up you living with me in front of your friends," Garrett said that night as we laid in what had been his perfectly-made bed . . . before we had messed it up.

"It's okay. I didn't mean to freeze. I just didn't know what to say." I still didn't.

"You practically already live here. I mean, you stay with me most nights of the week. Fizzy and Babbitt get along perfectly."

I looked over the side of the bed where Fizzy—my pit bull mix—and Babbitt—Garrett's Alaskan Malamute—lay with their heads on each other's backs. They loved each other.

"I know. You're right." I ran my fingers over his waxed chest. "I just don't know if I'm ready to move in. It's a big step."

He rubbed my back. "I won't push, but the offer stands. You wouldn't even have to pay rent." His lips warmed the tip of my nose, and I wanted to blurt out, okay, I'll move in! But for some reason, the words wouldn't form.

"Thank you," I finally managed to say.

"Do you think this case you're helping Nikki with will be dangerous?"

"Nah. Honestly, I don't think it's a case at all. Alex probably ran away after breaking up with his girlfriend. I'm sure he'll turn up soon."

Garrett nodded and pushed a strand of hair behind my ear. "You're beautiful."

I could feel the blush overtaking my face.

"I think you're the most beautiful woman I've ever met." His gaze searched me, taking in everything. "I still can't believe you agreed to go on a second date with me after I acted so badly on our first date."

He had gotten completely drunk, and I'd had to drive him home.

"I'm glad I did," I said.

Everything about him was basically perfect. He was handsome, tall, had a fantastic job, and loved his family to a fault. So why did I feel nauseous every time I thought about being in a serious long-term relationship with him?

I kissed him on the cheek and rolled out of bed. Fizzy looked up, and I patted him on the head.

"Everything okay?" Garrett asked.

"Yep, I just need to use the restroom." And take a breather.

I closed the bathroom door behind me and tried to calm the anxiety rising in my chest. I turned on the faucet and splashed cold water on my face.

This was stupid. I knew how to be in a long-term relationship. I'd stayed in one with a complete and utter jerk for five years.

The mirror showed a more put-together version of myself than my insides felt. I needed to go home—to my parents' home—for the night. I needed to get my thoughts together.

I opened the door ready to tell Garrett I had to leave, only to almost run straight into him.

"Don't freak out." He wrapped his muscular arms around me in a bear hug. "I didn't mean to go so fast. It was an impulsive offer."

The tightness in my chest loosened a bit.

"If you want to go home tonight, I understand."

How could he have known that's what I was thinking?

"But I wish you'd stay."

My hands shook. "I'll stay."

He bent down and kissed the top of my head. "Also, your phone buzzed while you were in there." He pointed to the nightstand on the side of the bed where I usually slept. "I didn't look, I promise."

I smiled up at him and kissed his lips. "I have nothing to hide."

"You're entitled to your privacy, though."

We got back in bed, and I opened the message on my phone. It was from Nikki.

My Uncle's snowmobile is missing.

As in Alex's dad's?

Yes. I need you to meet me right now.

The clock said two in the morning. I was exhausted after training and movie night and finding a teenage popsicle on the beach.

Can it wait until tomorrow? Please?

No. Now.

I clicked the phone off.

"I have to go. Nikki needs me," I said not believing those words had come out of my mouth.

I leaned down and kissed him long and hard.

"What was that for?" he asked when we separated.

"An apology, I guess," I said with a wink. "I'll be back as soon as Nikki is done with me. Don't wait up."

His eyes were already partially closed. "Okay."

I yanked on my jeans and tennis shoes the whole time yearning to be in the warm bed snuggled up next to Garrett.

The address Nikki texted me was eerily close to where we'd had snowmobile training the day before. Pieces of this puzzle were slowly starting to click together in my mind.

"I'm so glad you're here," Nikki said meeting me at my car. "My Aunt Elaine called and told me she'd found the snowmobile missing. She thinks Alex may have taken it."

"Can I talk to her?" I asked.

Nikki nodded and led me inside. The house was larger than average with modern fixtures.

A woman with the same long auburn hair as Nikki invited us to sit on her white sofas.

"Thank you so much for coming, Rylie," Elaine said.

"I'm happy to be here." I hoped the smile I'd plastered on my face was convincing enough. "Can you tell me a little bit about what happened?"

"I found the snowmobile missing tonight. I couldn't sleep so I thought I'd walk around and I found myself out in the auxiliary garage." She was rubbing a circle into one hand with the thumb of the other. "I don't know how I even ended up in there. But that's when I noticed one of the snowmobiles was missing."

"And what about last night? Do you remember anything out of the ordinary about Alex?"

Her thumb rubbing stopped. "It was a normal night," she said looking at the fire in the fireplace instead of me. "Alex went out with Jordan and Debbie, and I heard him come back around eleven or so."

On the end table next to me was a photograph of three boys. "Are these all of your boys?" I asked.

She looked over at the photo and smiled. "Yes. Hal Junior is going to school for engineering at Mining College. Alex had considered that school in addition to several others. He's been offered scholarships all across the country to play football. And Henry is the youngest. He's only ten, but he keeps me busy with all of his sports."

"They're all so handsome," I said trying to break the ice a bit more.

"Thank you." She beamed with pride.

"Do they get along?" I asked. "My sister and I have had some gnarly fights over the years."

"I had a sister too," she said smiling at Nikki. "Boys are so much different. Their fights are intense but short-lived. And my boys really love each other. They're always looking out for one another."

"Would you mind if I took a look around the auxiliary garage?" I asked.

"Not at all." She stood and walked us down to the

68

basement where the garage opened up to their back yard. "He took a helmet too, thank goodness."

"Only one helmet?" I asked.

She nodded. "The others are all here."

So much for him running off with a girlfriend.

"And he's pretty experienced on these?" I asked.

"He's been on them since he could walk. Before football, we actually considered getting him into snowmobile racing."

"I remember when we were up in Togwotee, and he used to challenge me to races," Nikki said. "He always won."

"Speed is his thing," Elaine said. "He's always been my little cheetah." Her gaze became distant. "Do you think he's okay?"

"I'm sure he's fine," Nikki said. "We're going to find him."

"Elaine?" A deep voice came from the stairs.

Elaine's face paled. "Down here," she said closing the door to the garage.

A man I'd only seen once before—at the uniform shop —stood wearing a badge exactly like the one Luke wore.

"This is my husband, Hal," Elaine said.

"What's going on?" he asked. "Why are you up at this time of night?"

"I couldn't sleep so I was walking around and found Alex's snowmobile missing," Elaine explained.

"Why didn't you call me?" he asked, his tone the same angry one as at the uniform shop. "Nikki's just a park ranger. She can't help the same way I can."

Nikki looked down at her shoes but said nothing.

"I didn't want to bother you if it was nothing," Elaine said.

"It sure as hell isn't nothing. Our son is missing, and you find a snowmobile gone." He took a step toward her. She took a step back. "Don't you think those two things have something to do with one another?"

"Why don't we go talk upstairs," Elaine said.

He huffed and turned back up the stairs.

"I'll be right back." Elaine smiled at us, apparently embarrassed by her husband's behavior.

"Your uncle is . . . intense," I said when they had disappeared up the stairs.

"He's an ass," Nikki said.

"Psst," a whisper came from behind us.

Nikki turned. "Henry? Have you been spying on us this whole time?" She smiled and ruffled his hair.

"Did you find Alex?" he asked, his big brown eyes full of hope.

"Not yet," Nikki said. "But we're not going to give up."

"Do you remember anything about the night Alex disappeared?" I asked.

He looked down at his feet.

"It's okay, you can tell her," Nikki said.

"Dad and Alex got into a big fight," he said.

"About what?" Nikki asked.

"Alex said he didn't want to play football anymore." Henry looked over toward the garage. "Then he left."

"On the snowmobile?" I asked.

"No. He didn't take that until later."

"Do you know where he might have gone when he left?" Nikki asked.

Henry shrugged.

"But you saw him take the snowmobile?" I asked.

"I heard it," he said.

"What time was that?" I didn't mean to give the kid the third degree, but he seemed to know more than anyone else did at this point.

"Five in the morning. I was mad he woke me up."

"Does he take the snowmobile a lot?" Nikki asked.

"Sometimes." He shrugged again. "But don't tell Mom and Dad. They don't know."

"I promise," I said. "Has Alex been acting normal lately? Other than not wanting to play football anymore?"

"Yeah. I think so," Henry said. "Here come my parents. Don't tell them I talked to you."

Footsteps on the stairs led to the not-so-happy couple's reappearance. When I turned back to look at Henry, he wasn't there anymore.

"Did you and Alex get into an argument the night he went missing?" Nikki asked, her hands on her hips.

Elaine's eyes were huge.

"Where did you hear that?" He looked at his wife.

"She didn't tell me. I just thought maybe—"

"Nothing out of the ordinary," Hal said. "Just a normal father-son argument."

Elaine didn't make eye contact with either of us.

"I think we need to get a search team out looking for Alex," I said trying to break the tension. "If he left on a snowmobile, we could possibly follow his tracks. It hasn't snowed in the past couple of days."

"The forecast says we're going to get snow tonight," Nikki said.

"Then we should get going now." My brain was practically begging to go back to sleep, but if we had a shot at finding Alex, this was it.

"I'll call the search and rescue unit," Hal said.

"And we'll call the rangers," I said. "I have a feeling I know where he went."

11

G arrett was still in bed when I got back to his place. I'd gone back to get my uniform and duty bag and give Fizzy and Babbitt big hugs.

By the time I reached the meadow where we'd had training, it was swarming with police and park rangers.

"We'll go on snowmobile," Greg said. "Do you still have the drone?" He was talking to a police officer I hadn't seen before.

"The drone batteries will only last fifteen to twenty minutes in this cold," he said. "But we'll see what we can do."

The sun was just starting to peek over the horizon, but the clouds were ominous. If it snowed, we'd lose any chance at following Alex's trail.

"Rylie, do you remember seeing tracks near that meadow we found disturbed?" Greg asked.

I pulled out my phone and showed him the photo of the tracks leading into the trees.

"Do you think you could find those tracks again?"

"Definitely," I replied.

He handed me a helmet. "We'll follow you."

I led the way through the powder that still looked the same as it had after we'd had training. The site where we'd cleaned up empty beer cups and put out the fire was easy to find. I stopped on the hill and searched the tree line to find Alex's tracks again. The drone circled overhead.

I pointed to where the tracks were and started down the hill toward them. Four or five snowmobiles followed me. Three for sure were rangers. The others were the search and rescue part of the fire department.

The tracks wound through the trees and up the mountainside. I went as fast as I could without losing everyone or hitting a tree. How Alex had done this in the dark was beyond me.

It had to have been ten miles up the mountain before we found where the tracks ended.

I stopped my sled and jumped off.

Alex's snowmobile was lodged in a tree trunk. Its skis were mangled, the fiberglass hood shattered. I turned three-sixty looking for Alex but saw nothing.

"Where is he?" Greg called out from behind me. "Do you see him?"

I ran through the snow as quickly as I could toward the twisted pile of machine.

Footprints and a trail of blood led to the south.

"Come on." After that accident, Alex couldn't have gotten far. If all that blood belonged to him, I was afraid of what we might find. Thankfully, Nikki had stayed back at incident command.

Greg called out over the radio on the channel designated for the search. "We have footprints and blood. We're going to need to have an ambulance ready."

"Copy," the officer in charge said.

The footprints turned to more of a crawling, blood tainting the pristine snow. And then at the end of the path, twenty yards ahead of me, was a body.

I don't know how, but my legs propelled me forward even faster.

It was Alex. He still wore his helmet, but the visor was shattered.

I yanked off my glove and reached two fingers up under the helmet. Tears stung at my eyes.

"Please be alive, please be alive," I whispered.

Finally, a tiny beat hit my fingertips.

"He has a pulse," I yelled over my shoulder. "Bring the backboard."

Two firefighters came up beside me.

"Don't move him. Do not take off the helmet," I instructed.

They nodded. They knew that. Of course, they knew that.

"We have to get him out of here quickly."

"You should pull him," one of the firefighters said. "You know the area the best and you led us in."

"Fine," I agreed. "We'll hook up the backboard sled to my snowmobile and I'll pull him out."

We got him rolled onto the backboard—stabilizing his head and neck—and strapped him down.

Once he was in the sled and secured to my snowmobile, I jumped on.

"Follow me and watch him," I said. "If something happens, get my attention, and I'll stop."

They nodded, and we all took off. When we arrived back at the parking lot and incident command, Nikki rushed to Alex's side.

"Don't move him," I said.

"Alex," Nikki sobbed. "Wake up."

"We need to get him into the ambulance and to the hospital," I said.

Luke appeared at our side. "Get in my squad car. I'll take you."

She kissed Alex on the cheek and ran to Luke's car sliding into the front seat. "You can come too," she called back to me.

"Do I get to sit in the back?" I tried at a joke, but it didn't come out funny.

"Unless you want to drive." Luke smiled.

"Can you take care of the sled and everything?" I asked Ben as the paramedics were getting Alex into the ambulance.

"Yes. Just take care of Nikki," he said. "You're two for two now. You found two alive bodies." He patted me on the back.

I handed him my helmet and followed Luke to the car.

Nikki was on the phone when we got in.

"They're taking him to North-Central Hospital now. He has a pulse, but he's unconscious." Her voice was wobbly but clear. "We'll meet you there."

She hung up. "That was Aunt Elaine."

The ambulance pulled out with lights and sirens blazing.

Luke turned on his lights too and followed closely behind.

The doctors whisked Alex away the moment we arrived leaving Luke, Nikki, and I in a small waiting room.

"I can't believe we found him," Nikki said to no one but herself as she paced the room.

Luke kept checking his cell phone.

The adrenaline had finally worn off, and my eyelids felt heavy. Before I knew it, Nikki was shaking me awake.

"Did I fall asleep?" I asked, my voice raspy.

"It's okay," Nikki said. "He's okay."

"Alex?" I asked standing up. "How long was I asleep?"

"A couple of hours," Nikki said. We were the only two in the waiting room. "Do you want to go see him?" Her sense of urgency had evaporated leaving a much calmer Nikki.

"Is he awake?" I asked.

She shook her head. "The doctor said he could be unconscious for a while."

"Okay," I said. "But first, let's discuss where we're at with all of this."

"We know what happened to Jordan and what happened to Alex probably happened at the same time, so Alex couldn't have done it."

My brain was still fuzzy with sleep, but I knew that wasn't entirely true. "If Alex left at five in the morning, he definitely could have done something to Jordan before."

Nikki scowled. "Whose side are you on?"

"I'm not on a side. I just want to find out what happened," I said. "We know that there was a party in the field. There was drinking. Debbie, Jordan, and Alex were all together at the reservoir before they went to the party. Debbie and Alex looked perfectly happy at that point. Jordan didn't."

"He was always jealous of Alex," Nikki said.

"Then they went to the party."

"And Alex broke up with Debbie."

"Or so she says," I said.

"Do you think she was lying?"

"She was definitely lying about something, but I don't know exactly what."

"Maybe she did all of this," Nikki said.

"It's possible," I said slowly. "But it would have been a pretty intricate plan to hurt both boys."

Nikki sighed. "Okay, so then Alex left the party and went home."

"And got into an argument with his dad."

"And then left."

"For several hours," I said.

"Before he came back for the snowmobile." Nikki slid into a chair. "Oh my goodness. What if he did do this to Jordan? He had plenty of time."

"We don't know that. Maybe he went back to the party," I said. "We definitely need to fill in some of the blanks. Where do you think he was going on the snowmobile?" I asked.

"Nowhere," Nikki said. "He was probably just riding to clear his head. He did that a lot when he and his dad got into arguments on our vacations."

"They argue a lot?" I asked.

"Always have. Uncle Hal has high expectations of Alex."

"What about the other boys?" I asked.

"He doesn't pay them much attention," she said.

I tried to process all of this. "So who are our suspects?"

"Debbie. And Alex," she whispered. "Either of them could have done something to Jordan."

"What about your uncle?" I asked. "If he thought Jordan might take Alex's position as starting quarterback, would he do something like this?"

She shook her head slowly. "He's a police officer."

"And?" I asked. We both knew wearing a badge didn't make someone perfect.

She groaned. "I don't know. All of this is just awful."

I didn't want to push any further, but I added him to my mental suspect list.

When we walked into Alex's room, a pretty red-headed woman hugged Nikki.

"Hey, Mom," Nikki said. "Dad."

A man who was probably six foot seven draped his arm around Nikki's shoulder. "How you doing kid?"

"Hanging in there. This is Rylie. From the reservoir." Nikki motioned to me.

"It's a pleasure to meet you, Rylie. We've heard a lot about you," Nikki's mom said.

I'm sure they had.

"You're the one who used to date—" her dad started, but her mom jabbed him in the ribs. "Right. You're the one who just got the full-time position."

"That's me," I said with a smile.

"And you know my aunt." Nikki motioned to Elaine who sat in a chair next to Alex's bed, holding his blue hand.

The resemblance between the three women was striking. They all had long red hair and perfect porcelain skin. Their makeup was flawless, their nails chip-free.

I shoved my hands in my pockets to hide my plain, non-manicured fingers.

"Where's Uncle Hal?" Nikki asked looking around at the other faces.

"He had an errand to run." Her aunt didn't look up from her son's face. "He should be back soon."

I struggled to keep a neutral expression. What kind of father didn't sit at his son's bedside?

"Here, have a seat," Nikki's mom said pulling up two chairs for us.

The family made small talk, mostly about the yacht club and the comings and goings of people I didn't know. Every once in a while they'd talk about Luke, and my ears would perk up, but it was obvious they were being extra careful around me knowing our history.

When it had been at least an hour, more people began to show up. As in, every single student from the local high school.

One at a time, they came in, squeezed Alex's hand or said a couple of words, then tearfully left the room. Some prayed. Some gave him hugs. Most knew his mom, and she welcomed them all warmly.

When they were finished, they formed chatty groups in

the hallways. I was surprised the nurses didn't tell them to leave.

"Should we talk to some of these kids?" I asked Nikki when her family was distracted by their conversation. "See if they know anything?"

"We should before Luke gets back."

When we walked into the hall, one of the cheerleaders —she was still in her uniform—ran over to me. "Are you the one who found Alex?"

"Yes," I said.

"Thank you so much for saving him," she gushed. The rest of the group nodded with big smiles on their faces.

I decided to take advantage of this moment of popularity. "Can I talk to you about something?"

She looked a bit confused but nodded. "Here or—"

"Let's go down the hall." I led her out of earshot of the rest of them. "I'm just trying to figure out what could have happened to Alex. And Jordan, of course."

"What do you think happened? Do you think they're related?" She spoke so fast it was almost hard to understand her.

"I don't know. I'm not a cop, but I like to figure things out. It's kind of in my blood."

She smiled.

"So do you know anything about the party a couple of nights ago? There was a fire and some drinking." I quickly added, "Don't worry, I'm not going to say anything about the drinking."

She hesitated. "I heard there was a party."

Smart girl. Not incriminating herself.

"I think Debbie and Alex went there together," she

said. "But he broke up with her in front of everyone." She said the last part at a whisper.

"That's terrible," I feigned shock.

"She deserved it, if you ask me." She looked down at her nails. "Alex was a catch, and she treated him like dirt."

"Do you know why he broke up with her?"

"He said something about changing his life—going a new direction." She stopped herself. "I mean, that's what I heard from someone anyway."

"Did you hear anything else about the party?"

She shook her head. "Nope. But hold on. Let me get Doryan." She half-jogged down the hall and grabbed one of the other girls. "You were at the party, right?" she asked the girl.

Doryan stared at her.

"Don't worry, she's not going to say anything."

"Uh, yeah. I was at the party. You saw me there," Doryan said. I guess she figured if she was going down, her friend would go down with her.

The girl in the cheerleading outfit blushed. "Can you tell her if you saw anything strange happen? With Alex?"

"I didn't see Alex there," Doryan said.

"You didn't see Alex there? Didn't you see the breakup?"

I stood quietly and listened to them talk.

Doryan shook her head. "I got there late. Debbie and Jordan were hanging out by the time I got there."

"Were Debbie and Jordan together the rest of the night?" I asked.

Doryan shrugged. "Don't know. I don't really keep tabs on them. I was preoccupied with my own stuff."

"She has a boyfriend," the girl in the cheerleading outfit said as if that justified everything.

"Do you know anyone else who was there?" I asked.

Doryan nodded. "Basically everyone standing over there." She pointed to the group of people watching us from the corners of their eyes. "Jase, come over here," she yelled.

A boy who looked younger than the two girls walked over. "Yeah?"

"She's trying to figure out what happened to Alex and Jordan. You were at the party. Did you see anything strange?"

Jase looked like he might vomit.

"It's okay. I'm not a cop. I don't really care what you were doing."

He nodded. "Jordan and Alex were together most of the night."

"No. Alex left," the cheerleader said. "After he and Debbie broke up."

Jase shook his head. "No. I know I saw them drinking together. I didn't see Debbie at all."

Doryan rolled her eyes. "You were probably too drunk to realize what was going on."

"I wasn't too drunk to see the awesome snowmobile show," Jase said.

"Snowmobile show?" I asked.

"Right as the party was dying down, a snowmobile came out of nowhere doing tricks, jumping over snow banks, and racing around like nobody's business."

Doryan gasped. "That was Alex wasn't it?"

"It could have been. It makes the most sense," I said. "What time did this snowmobiler show up?"

"Probably three or four in the morning," Jase said. "I don't know. I was pretty drunk."

"Did anyone see who Jordan left with?" I asked the three of them.

They all shook their heads. "Hey," Doryan yelled to the group. "Any of you see who Jordan left with after the party?"

The teenagers looked shocked that she was yelling about an illegal party in the presence of adults.

"He left with me," Debbie said walking up next to Doryan. She wore her cheerleading outfit with the leather jacket over top and held a handbag bedazzled with tiny stars that probably cost more than a month's rent on that apartment. "I took him home. He was too drunk to drive."

Everyone stared at her.

"Why didn't you tell me this before?" I asked.

"It didn't seem important or whatever," Debbie challenged.

"So you were the last person to see Jordan before he ended up half-naked on the frozen beach?"

Debbie shrugged. "I guess. But why does that matter? Jordan was an idiot. He probably undressed and walked to the beach."

"Does he live near there?" I asked.

"He could have driven." She shrugged.

Except we hadn't found his car.

"Did anything happen between you and Jordan?" I asked.

"Of course not. I'd just broken up with his best friend."

"Um, pretty sure he broke up with you," Doryan said.

"Yeah." Another boy from the group walked over. "And I totally saw you and Jordan making out in your car before you left."

Debbie's cheeks flushed. "You don't know anything. You were all drunk."

She turned and stomped back down the hallway.

"I'm sorry," a doctor said in the doorway of the room. "I'm going to need everyone besides the patient's mother to step out of the room, please."

I turned toward Nikki with a questioning look. She looked terrified.

"My family can stay too, right?" Elaine asked in a small voice.

"If you'd like them to, yes," the doctor said slowly.

What was she going to tell them? Was Alex going to die?

Nikki and her mother and father joined Elaine in the room while I stayed in the hallway with the teenage entourage.

"Why weren't all of you at Jordan's bedside?" I asked Jase.

"Jordan's a douche," Jase said. "No one likes him. He's always just been Alex's tag-along."

"Do you think Jordan did that to himself?" I asked.

Doryan shook her head. "He was an idiot, especially when he was drunk, but to strip down and lay on a frozen beach and nearly die? Even he's not that stupid."

Alcohol made people do crazy things. I'd seen it way

too many times on the fire department. And it made you think you were warm when your body was freezing. It was plausible he had done it to himself. But how did he get there? His feet weren't torn up, and he wasn't wearing shoes.

When Alex's door opened Nikki stood on the other side, her face paler than usual.

"What did the doctor say?" I asked but Nikki's eyes locked onto the group of teenagers.

"Which one of you punks gave Alex drugs?"

12

The entire hallway was silent, everyone waiting for someone else to say something.

"I know it was one of you." Nikki pointed her finger.

"That's enough, Nikole," Nikki's dad said in a deep voice.

Nikki's fury turned to tears as she leaned into her dad.

"Do you know why Alex would have been taking drugs?" I asked Doryan quietly.

"Alex never took drugs," Doryan said. "He knew it would get him kicked off the team."

But if he didn't want to be on the team anymore . . .

"Plus, after Barry died a few years ago, Alex swore to never do drugs. Barry was his best friend, before Jordan."

"Maybe he'd had a bad night and decided to take something?" I offered.

She shook her head. "If he had drugs in his system, someone put them there." She looked around at the others. "Do you think it was one of them?"

"It could have been. Or it could have been completely unrelated."

"But it probably happened at the party, right?" she asked.

"It seems likely," I admitted.

She wrapped her arms around her. "I knew those parties were a bad idea."

"Who would have wanted Alex dead?" I asked.

"Dead?" Jase asked. "I don't think anyone wanted to kill Alex. I mean, who would have known he would have gotten on a snowmobile and driven it all over the place?"

He had a point. "Then what do you think it was."

"Isn't it obvious?" he asked.

My head hurt, and I was exhausted. Nothing was obvious right now.

"Football. If he even had a trace of drugs in his system, he would be kicked off the team," Jase said.

"Jordan," Doryan and I both said at the same time.

Jase nodded. "He had the most to gain from Alex getting booted. Especially with the championship game coming up."

"They'll have to cancel it now," Doryan said. "We don't have a third quarterback."

"Can you please tell me where Alex Ward is?" A girl with an unkempt braid of mousy brown hair and glasses asked at the nurse's station.

The nurse pointed to Alex's door as if it were obvious.

No one seemed to notice her slip into the room. Elaine, Nikki, and Nikki's parents were huddled together talking to the doctor. The other teenagers seemed unlikely to notice someone who wasn't part of their clique.

"Thanks for your help," I said.

When I walked in the room, the girl was sitting where Elaine had been, holding Alex's hand with her forehead on the bed beside him. She looked like she was praying as her body jerked with every sob.

"It wasn't supposed to be this way. We were supposed to go to college together," she whispered. "Why would you do this?"

"Why would he do what?" I asked quietly so as not to startle her too much.

She stood dropping Alex's hand and pushing her glasses up on her nose. "Nothing. I'm sorry. I shouldn't even be here."

Before I could get her name, she pushed past me and disappeared down the hallway.

"Who was that?" I asked Doryan when I came back out.

"Who was who?" she asked.

Ugh. Popular kids.

I ran down the hallway after the girl. If nothing else, I'd catch her in the parking lot. She seemed to have more information than anyone else.

I punched the elevator numbers over and over again as if it would help the elevator come more quickly.

When the silver doors opened, Luke stepped out. "Hey, Ry."

I didn't have time to talk to him. "I have to go. I'll be back in a minute."

"Hold on," he said. "What's the rush?"

"I need to speak with someone who just went down on

the last elevator." I punched the ground floor button on the inside wall. "I'll come right back."

Luke nodded and moved his hand from preventing the doors from closing.

The lobby was empty when I got off the elevator. I ran outside only to find the girl in the glasses driving away in a silver Jetta. Her eyes widened when she saw me chasing after her and hit the gas.

Before I could get a full license plate number, she turned the corner nearly spinning out on the ice. The first two letters were K and H. It shouldn't be too hard to find her car at the high school. I'd catch up with her later.

Luke had his arm wrapped around Nikki when I got back upstairs. "Did you find who you were looking for?"

"No," I said. "She got away."

"Please tell me you're not investigating," Luke said.

"I'm not investigating?" I said.

"You're a terrible liar," Luke said. "What have you found out?"

"Maybe we should talk somewhere else," I said looking around at the teenagers. "I need a ride back to my car anyway."

"Me too," Nikki said.

I sat in the back again, not that I would have dared try and take the front from Nikki. I thought she was going to punch me when I'd asked Luke for a ride back to my car. So much for not being jealous.

We told Luke everything we knew. I may have left out

what I heard from the girl in glasses, but that wasn't anything . . . yet.

"What about you?" I asked. "Do you have any information?"

"When Nikki texted me about the drugs in Alex's system, I had the rangers pull the trash bags with the cups from the dumpster. We're going to run them and see if there are any traces of drugs inside. If we find drugs, we'll be able to deduce that he ingested them at the party. The phone message with the girl sobbing was a dead end. We couldn't trace the number."

Luke didn't say anything about him being drugged, just that he would have ingested them.

"The best thing we can hope for is that both Jordan and Alex wake up and tell us what happened."

Nikki stared out the window. "I still think it was Debbie. She gave him the drugs. She was mad that he broke up with her and wanted to ruin his life."

"I think Jordan had more to gain from Alex's fall from grace," I said.

"But how did Jordan end up as a victim as well?" Luke asked.

I shrugged. Nothing was clear. Nothing was easy. "I think we should talk to Dave."

"Jerry and I already talked to him. I know." He held up a hand. "I said you could come with us, but you were a bit preoccupied."

"And? Did he say anything?" I asked, my voice less irritated than I felt.

"Just that he saw some lights from outside the gate. He was driving by or something," Luke said. "He was lying, obviously, but that's all we could get out of him."

"What time did he see the lights?" I asked.

"Three or four in the morning," Luke said.

Nikki and I looked at one another.

"Then Alex couldn't be responsible for what happened to Jordan," Nikki said.

"Unless someone isn't giving us the entire story. What happened to Jordan could have been quick," Luke said.

Nikki crossed her arms over her chest.

"But you're probably right," he said quickly. "I don't think Alex had anything to do with what happened to Jordan. Not directly anyway."

Luke and Jerry may not have had luck talking to Dave, but I would. Every part of my body was screaming for rest, but this was more important. I'd rest right after I talked to Dave.

D ave was where he was every day. In his pop-up ice fishing tent in Muddy Water Cove.

I announced myself before unzipping the flap. "Dave, it's Rylie—the park ranger. I'm off duty, but I want to chat with you."

"Yeah, come in."

I stepped inside where a bead of sweat instantly appeared on my forehead. I pulled off my beanie and smoothed down my hair. "It's hot in here. Aren't you afraid you'll melt the ice and fall through?"

"Not as afraid as you, apparently." He snickered at the huge float coat I wore. A float coat is a personal floatation device built into a jacket made to keep you warm and safe on the ice.

"I already talked to the police," Dave said. "I wasn't trespassing."

"They told me that's what you said. But come on, Dave." I raised my eyebrows.

"I saw some lights. That's it."

"Where were you when you saw the lights?" I asked.

"I was outside the gate, of course."

I crossed my arms over my chest. "Dave, you know the only reason you're not in jail right now is because of me, right?"

"Yeah, I heard something from Carmen but—"

"And that I almost died trying to clear your name?"

"Yeah, yeah."

"So I'm going to ask again." I channeled my best cop voice. "Where were you when you saw the lights? I'm not going to do anything about it, I just need to know."

Dave looked down into the hole where his fishing line was motionless. "I may have been somewhere I shouldn't have been."

Finally, we were getting somewhere. "And can you tell me anything else about what you saw?"

"There were people on the ice."

"How many?"

"I don't know. Two? Three? Five."

"Where were they exactly?"

He pointed toward the center of the reservoir. "Out in the middle somewhere. They came from that walk-in gate." He pointed in the direction of the gate nearest Marina Cove.

"And what were they doing?" I asked.

"They were being idiots. Running around with their flashlights yelling and screaming. One was definitely a man, he was yelling like nobody's business."

"Like panicked yells or happy yells?"

"How am I supposed to know? Honestly, I thought it was you guys at first, so I took all my stuff and was getting ready to make a run for it, but then I realized it was probably just some stupid kids. I left anyway because I figured they'd be called in and I didn't want to be caught as well."

"Why didn't you call them in?"

"That's a little hypocritical, don't you think?"

"Do you think it's safe being on the ice at night?" I asked.

Dave raised an eyebrow. "Now you care about my safety?"

"I care about everyone's safety. I'd hate to come in and find you like I found—"

"Stop worrying so much. The ice is solid. It's been freezing cold." He stomped his foot in the inch of slush he'd created from his heater.

I shook my head. "Let me know if you remember anything else. And stay out of the reservoir at night."

───────

When I walked into my parent's house, the only thing I could think about was a warm bath and sleep—not necessarily in that order.

"Did you hear about the teenagers they found in the parks?" Mom asked. The news was on in the background, and Alex's football picture filled the TV screen.

"I found them. Both of them," I said.

My father turned from his chair and looked at me. Mom's mouth was partially open.

"Are you okay?" Mom asked when she finally snapped out of her momentary shock.

"It's been a crazy couple of days," I said. "I'm tired."

"They said he'd been doing drugs." She returned to stirring a big pot of soup on the stove.

"We're just trying to figure out if he did this to himself or if someone did it to him," I said.

She stopped stirring. "What do you mean if someone did it to him?" Panic flooded her eyes. "You don't think this was another crime? You're not *investigating* another crime, right?"

"It's not the same as the last one."

Or the one before that.

"It's some sort of weird high school drama. I'm not going to get hurt. I promise."

She eyed me up and down and then changed the subject. "Did you say you have to work Christmas Eve?"

We had been over my schedule no less than five times. Each time I told her I had to work Christmas Eve and each time she'd given me a guilt trip about it.

"I do, but I'll be home by eight. The boys don't even go to bed until ten so we can do our one gift when I get here."

"What about dinner?" she asked.

"You can eat without me. Just save me some of your famous stuffing." I smiled. Flattery usually helped these situations.

"What about Garrett? Is his mother coming into town?"

I hadn't even thought to talk to Garrett about his plans. "I don't know."

"If he doesn't have plans, invite him to dinner. He's welcome even if you're not here."

"I'll make sure to do that." Sometimes I thought my mother liked Garrett more than I did. But she also liked Luke.

"Tonight. Ask him tonight."

"Okay. I'll ask him tonight."

"It's only a week away. He's probably wondering why you haven't brought it up."

"He hasn't either," I said defensively. "We didn't spend Thanksgiving together."

"You weren't practically living together in November." She raised her eyebrows and smiled.

"We're not living together."

"Oh, I know you're not *officially*." She did air quotes with her fingers. "All of your stuff still lives in our basement. But it's just a matter of time."

No, it wasn't. The tightness in my chest returned. "I think I'm going to go take a nap."

I woke with a start when my cell phone buzzed next to my ear. I'd been dreaming of Garrett proposing and me running away.

Stupid, Rylie. He's perfect.

It was a number I didn't recognize.

I know what happened with Alex. Meet me tonight at the bar on 15th and Fern at 7pm. Come alone.

My heart pounded against my ribs. The last time

someone had told me to come alone, it'd ended in a big mess. I needed to know more.

Without thinking, I did something I hated doing. I clicked on the phone number and put the phone to my ear.

It began ringing. Was the person on the other end freaking out? Would they answer?

I waited for a voicemail. That would tell me who it was at least. But when it stopped ringing, the pre-programmed message with the robot lady voice and the phone number was all I got. Dammit. It was worth a shot.

I hung up.

Why are you calling me?

The message popped up on the screen within seconds.

Who is this? I'm not going to meet you unless I know who this is.

I'd been in enough dangerous situations since becoming a park ranger.

Then we won't meet.

Poop. They called my bluff.

Fine. Don't tell me. I'll be there.

At least it was at a public bar. What was the worst that could happen?

14

I showed up at seven o'clock on the dot. There were only two people in the bar—the bartender and a man with his back to me in a corner booth.

When I walked in, the man in the booth turned and waved. How he knew who I was, I didn't know since I'd never seen him before in my life.

"Are you the one I'm supposed to be meeting?" I asked.

He smiled. "I must be." He motioned around the room.

"Okay, so what do you have for me?"

"Wow, just getting down to it then?" He laughed. He was probably in his early twenties, a shiny black bald head, and deep brown eyes. "Can I at least buy you a beer?"

"Sure. Bud Light draft with limes."

"Got it." He stood up and walked to the bar. I shifted in my seat. I had really wanted to get in and get out. This guy was acting like we were on a date.

He walked back with my beer. I squeezed the limes in and took a sip. "Shall we get to business then?"

He laughed. "Well, I'm a receiver for the Denver Broncos."

I nearly spit out the beer in my mouth. "Wait, you're Marcus James, aren't you?" Apparently, I had seen him before.

"Very good. Are you a fan?"

I tried my best not to hyperventilate. Marcus James had my number and had actually texted me. "Definitely."

"That's good. It'd be pretty awkward if you were a Chiefs fan."

"So how do you know Alex?" I asked confused.

"Alex?" Marcus asked. The look on his face was of complete confusion. "Alex Holmes?"

"No. Alex Ward."

"I don't know an Alex Ward." He said. "I'm sorry, what did you say your name was?"

"Rylie. Rylie Cooper. You texted me earlier today about having information about Alex."

Marcus started laughing.

"You're not the one who texted me, are you?"

He shook his head slowly. "And you're not my blind date, are you?"

Now I was laughing. "Nope. I have a boyfriend."

"Too bad," he said with a devilish grin.

Was Marcus James flirting with me? "I should probably be going so when your date does get here, she doesn't find you having a drink with another woman."

"Wait. Tell me more about this Alex fellow," he said. "Maybe I can help."

I looked at the door.

"My date shouldn't be here for another half hour or so," he said.

"You're really early," I said.

"Just wanted to get comfortable." He smiled.

I was star struck.

It wasn't like I'd never met a football player before. I'd met Eli Hudson a few months ago and became good friends with his mom, coincidentally. But it wasn't like I hung out with Eli or any other football players from my favorite team.

"So who is Alex?" he asked.

"You've probably seen the news about the local quarterbacks from North-Central High who have been hospitalized?"

He nodded. "Okay, that Alex. So what? You're a cop?"

I shook my head. "A park ranger," I said. "Alex is one of my co-worker's cousins."

"Do they think someone did this to them?"

I didn't want to give away too much, but he was just so charming. "Maybe. And I think it has to do with football or girls or parents somehow."

"Sounds like the story of my high-school life." He laughed. "Well, besides the being hospitalized thing."

"It's just nothing makes sense." I took a drink of my beer. "Alex was a good kid. Didn't do drugs. Drank occasionally. But didn't want to play football anymore."

"Whoa. Stop there," Marcus said. "The star quarterback for the best high school team in the state didn't want to play football anymore?"

"That's what I've been told," I said.

"How did his parents take the news? My dad would have been pissed."

"His dad was angry," I said. "They got into a huge fight."

"I'd say you need to look into the dad first. That kid was going places. I'd heard rumors that he'd go pro within a year. If his parents were even slightly as obsessed about his career as mine were, they'd be my first suspect. Especially, with the second string quarterback who strategically —I mean, tragically—was injured too."

I felt like I'd swallowed a boulder. How was I going to tell Nikki that I thought her uncle could truly be a suspect?

"I should probably go," I said. "Enjoy your date."

He pulled out a card from his wallet. "Call me if you need to talk anything else over."

I nearly fainted. I had the personal phone number of a Denver Broncos football player.

"And I'll make sure to rub it in Eli's face that I got to have a beer with you." He laughed.

"Eli? As in Eli Hudson?" I asked.

"The minute you told me you were a park ranger, I knew exactly who you were. You're Eli's mom's friend."

"He talks about me?" How could this night get any weirder?

Marcus shrugged. "Once or twice."

I smiled. "Yes, please tell him I say hi." I made my way to another booth several steps away and positioned my back to Marcus to hide my smile.

I ordered a burger and another beer when the bartender came over to check on me. By the time my food arrived, an attractive young woman had joined Marcus at his booth.

I couldn't help overhear him telling her about our funny encounter. She didn't seem to think it was as amusing as he did and changed the subject rather quickly. Once I'd finished my burger, they were on their fourth drink, relaxed and laughing.

When they got up to leave I looked at my watch. It was nearly ten o'clock. I checked my phone. No texts.

"Hey, I hope this person shows," Marcus said as he walked by my table.

"Have a great night," I said to the two of them.

They smiled and left, arms wrapped around each other.

It was in that moment I longed to be in Garrett's arms. The thought surprised me, and I had to take a moment to evaluate it. Why wasn't I freaking out anymore? The knot in my chest had suddenly evaporated.

I pulled up my phone and texted Garrett.

If you're still up, I'll be there in about thirty minutes.

I was done waiting for whoever this was.
I texted them too.

I'm leaving.

Instantly I got a text back.

You didn't come alone.

What do you mean? I've been sitting here by myself all night.

No. You were with that football player.

I thought he was you.

I'm not a football player.

I wanted to text asking if they were a cheerleader, but decided against it.

Do you still want to meet tonight? I swear, I'm alone.

Can't now.

Damn.

Another time?

I was grasping at straws. This was ridiculous.

I'll contact you if I feel like I can trust you again.

I rolled my eyes and threw some money down on the table. What an utter waste of a night.

My phone buzzed again. Garrett.

The bed is nice and warm for you.

Maybe the night wasn't lost after all.

15

It was Saturday—both Garrett's and my day off—and we were sitting in front of the fireplace with our respective cups of coffee while he read the newspaper and I scrolled through various social apps on my phone. "I know it's less than a week away but do you have plans for Christmas Eve?" I asked Garrett.

He carefully folded the paper and laid it in his lap. "Now that I think about it, I don't." He took a sip of coffee. "Mom's coming into town Christmas Day, and we're going to visit Derrick together. But Christmas Eve is completely open."

"I have to work Christmas Eve, but my mom wanted me to invite you to dinner before I get off work, and then I'll be home, and we'll open one present."

"That's a fun tradition."

I smiled. "What traditions do you have for the holidays?"

Garrett thought for a while. "When I'm with my nonincarcerated brothers and their kids we always bake and decorate cookies and make snow angels. But I haven't really established any of my own."

"Maybe we need to fix that," I said and then instantly regretted it.

That was a fast-moving statement.

"Maybe we do," Garrett rubbed my foot that was in his lap. "I love you, Rylie."

The words tumbled out of his mouth as if it was something he'd said numerous times.

"I—" I sucked in as much air as my lungs would hold. "I love you too, Garrett."

Garrett smiled, his shoulders relaxing. "And yes, I'd love to come to Christmas Eve with your family, and you once you get off work."

"Perfect. I'll let my mom know." My heart was beating uncontrollably. A little smile formed on my lips.

I was in love.

I was terrified, but I was in love.

———

"He told you he loved you?" Shayla said later that day when we were all gathered at Seamus's place for the Avalanche game. Seamus, his roommates, and Garrett were on the couch watching the game unfold.

"And I said it back."

"You did?" The pitch of her voice raised an octave. "I'm so happy for you."

She hugged me. I tried to push away the niggling sense of anxiety that swelled in my chest just thinking about it.

"You and Seamus have said it too, right?" I asked.

"Yeah. He practically said it on our first date," Shayla said blushing.

"Do you think he'll propose?" I asked.

She shook her head. "No. We're taking things slow. He's been down that route before. It ended badly."

"He's been engaged?" I asked.

"Twice," Shayla said with a wince. "The first time was back in Ireland, right out of school. The other only about a year after he arrived here."

"Engaged twice. That's kind of a lot," I said trying to wrap my head around this new information.

Shayla shrugged. "He was young."

I took a sip of my beer.

"Have you found an apartment yet?"

"I haven't even looked. With everything going on, it's kind of gone to the back of my mind."

"And you don't want to live with Garrett?" she said. "Even though you've declared your love for each other?"

It was a solid thought. He probably thought that would be the next step. "No. I haven't changed my mind. I don't think we should live together quite yet."

"It's the cleanliness, isn't it?"

"It's exhausting." I sighed. "I feel like I leave a trail of filth behind me like that cute little kid from Charlie Brown."

"Pigpen?"

I nodded. "He was always my favorite."

"Are you really that dirty?" Shayla asked and then took a sip of her pink wine cooler.

"Not compared to normal standards. But in Garrett standards, I might as well be a garbage truck."

"Then why don't we get a place together?" Shayla asked. "We both want to move out of our parents' houses. You have a great job, and I'll have one soon."

This was perfect. Why hadn't I thought of it? "I think that's a great idea."

"Then I'll start looking. Academy is winding down with Christmas coming up, so I have some free time on my hands."

"If you need my help, let me know."

Shayla nodded. The guys in the living room cheered, standing and high-fiving each other. Garrett was even joining in on the fun.

"How's the investigation going with Nikki?"

"It's kind of stalled," I said. "I mean, I'm trying to chase down leads, but I ended up on a blind date with Marcus James—the Broncos player."

"How does that even happen?" She laughed.

I told her the story.

"I bet Nikki is beside herself over all of this," Shayla said.

"She is stuck between being devastated about her cousin's condition and trying to clear his name all at the same time," I said. "But I'm starting to wonder if it could be Alex's dad. Marcus actually brought it up. He said his parents were nuts about his football career and Alex's dad seems pretty nuts about it too."

"But why would he hurt Alex?" Shayla asked.

"I don't think he hurt Alex. I think he may have hurt Jordan."

"Why would he hurt Jordan?"

"Alex told his dad he didn't want to play football anymore. Probably that he'd let Jordan play in the championship game." I had been thinking about it all day.

"You think his dad took Jordan out so Alex would feel obligated to play?" Shayla asked.

I shrugged. "It makes a lot of sense. He's a cop. He has keys to our gates."

"Wait, he's a cop? What's his name?"

I hadn't even thought about the fact that Shayla probably knew of this guy. "Hal Ward."

She tipped her head back and let out a groan. "Alex is Officer Ward's son?"

"Yeah, does that mean something?"

Shayla looked me straight in the eye. "If anyone could have done it, Ward would be the man. He's crazy."

"And he's Nikki's uncle," I said as Nikki and Luke walked in the door.

"Hi. Did we miss much?" Nikki said.

Shayla nodded. We wouldn't be talking about it anymore.

"The game's a close one," Garrett said.

Luke took Nikki's jacket, grabbed a beer, and plopped down on the couch next to Seamus.

"Hey Nikki," Shayla said. "I'm so sorry about your cousin."

Nikki nodded. "Thanks." Then she turned to me. "Have you found anything?"

My heart did a flop. How was I going to tell her that I thought her uncle was my prime suspect? Even if she thought he was an ass, he was still her uncle.

"Not quite," I said. "I talked to Dave yesterday after you and I had coffee."

"And?"

"And he said he saw two or three or five people walking around on the ice yelling."

"Because they were all drunk," Nikki said. "Luke got the results back from the cups. There was only trace evidence of the drug that was in Alex's system."

"So not everyone got it," I concluded.

"Alex was drugged?" Shayla asked.

"Looks like someone put it in his beer." Nikki nodded. "Who knows if anyone else ingested it. But they didn't find any in Jordan's blood."

The three of us stood there in silence with our thoughts for a minute. And then the door opened again revealing Antonio and a gorgeous Asian woman.

"He has a girlfriend?" I blurted out.

"More like flavor of the week," Nikki said. "He's been going through them like candy since his divorce finalized. I thought he was a playboy while he was married, but now . . ." She shook her head.

Antonio's gaze scanned the room. When it landed on me, he instantly looked down at his date. "How about I introduce you to my friends?" he asked her.

She nodded and smiled up at him. He went around the room introducing everyone, but when he got to me, he didn't even look my way. "And that is Rylie," he said.

Her pretty smile drooped a bit. "Hello, Rylie." She shook my hand with crippling strength.

"Hi," I said. "It's nice to meet you."

Shayla must have noticed the wince on my face. "And I'm Shayla. I used to work with Antonio over the summer."

The woman let go of my hand and grabbed Shayla's with much less intensity. "It's wonderful to meet you."

"Can I get you anything to drink?" Shayla asked.

"I'd love a beer," the woman said. "Anything is fine."

Shayla returned with two beers handing one to Antonio who left his date with us and joined the guys on the couch.

"Tell us, what do you do?" Shayla, being the nice one of the three of us, asked while Nikki and I stood side by side, measuring this woman up.

After almost an hour of small talk, the game came to its second intermission, and I'd about had it with the glares I was getting from Antonio's date.

"You ready to go?" I asked Garrett bending over the back of the couch to whisper in his ear.

"Whenever you are," he turned and smiled up at me.

"Thanks for having us, Seamus," I said, and Garrett took the hint that we were actually leaving. Right now. He shook the guys' hands and helped me into my jacket kissing my cheek in the process.

When I handed Garrett his jacket, he turned to me and said, "Thanks, sweetie. I love you."

The entire room froze. The game was silent. All eyes were on me.

I didn't want to say it back.

Not here.

Not in front of Nikki and Luke and Antonio and . . .

But Garrett looked at me with his big lovable puppy dog eyes. And I did love him. Why would I try to hide it?

"I love you too," I said more hurriedly than I had meant, but Garrett didn't seem to notice. He pulled on his jacket, and we said our goodbyes while I ignored the startled expressions on my friends' faces.

16

Shayla never used punctuation in text messages unless it was to show emphasis. She said it was rude. I didn't care if it was rude, it was proper.

i can't believe you told him you loved him in front of everyone!!!!!!!

But I do love him. Why should I keep that a secret?

because everyone is freaking out!!!!

I sighed and clicked the phone off so the screen went dark.

"Is everything okay?" Garrett said from the driver's seat of his Corolla.

"Shayla's just telling me more about Antonio's date. Apparently, they won't leave." It was a harmless lie.

"She seemed nice from what I could tell."

"I think she was nice enough. Definitely Antonio's

type."

Garrett let out a nervous laugh. "You know, at one time I thought Antonio had a thing for you."

"I think he may have when I first started working at the reservoir," I admitted. "But it was likely because I was new and exciting. Now I'm rather old and—"

"You're not old," Garrett said. "You're young and beautiful and he'd be an idiot not to have a thing for you."

Was Garrett really offended a guy *didn't* have a thing for me?

"Either way, nothing ever happened with us, and I suspect nothing ever will."

"That's right because you're mine now." Garrett was only being nice, but the thought of being someone's made the tightness in my chest intensify.

My screen lit up, and I opened the messages app.

they can't stop talking about it
they can't believe you're in love so quickly

I rolled my eyes. What did they know? And didn't they have anything better to talk about? Like their own lives?

I sent back the shrugging girl emoji and clicked my phone off again.

It was the first mildly warm day since winter hit Colorado like a fast-moving freight train hitting a solid concrete wall. I didn't even need my long underwear when I opened the reservoir.

"Good morning, Carmen," I said when I walked into the office after finishing all of the opening procedures. "Hi, Antonio." I was more than surprised to see him, especially this early.

He grunted back without making eye contact.

"I hear you're in love," Carmen said ignoring Antonio's caveman act.

"Was there an email blast or something? Are you all on some kind of group text message?"

Carmen laughed. "Antonio told me."

I glanced over at him where he was still examining the intricate pattern of the carpet. Why had he been talking about me when he couldn't even look at me?

"Apparently, it was the talk of last night's party," Carmen continued oblivious.

"I bet it was," I murmured.

"It's the multiple personality guy, huh?" Carmen was the one who led me to the hypothesis that Garrett had multiple personalities when in reality he had a twin . . . and some anxiety that he occasionally took medication for.

Antonio's head shot up. "Multiple personalities?"

It was my turn to ignore him. "Garrett. His name is Garrett," I said. "And yes, I'm in love."

"Well, it looks good on you," Carmen said with a smile.

"Did Antonio tell you about his new girlfriend?" If he could stir the pot, so could I.

Carmen's eyes lit up. "A *girlfriend*?"

"She is not my girlfriend," Antonio said.

"You brought her to meet all your friends. Sounds

pretty serious to me." I shrugged.

Antonio's cheeks flushed.

"So tell me all about her," Carmen said. "Is she tall? Short? Does she have any pets?"

I shook my head and walked away. Carmen could take it from here.

───────────

Midway through my shift Carmen called on my cell and told me that Nikki's and my vests were ready to be picked up. Since there were two other rangers in the office, I was free to pick them up.

"There you are. I can't believe how quickly they came in," Michelle said when I walked back to the back of the store. She pulled them from a rack behind her. "Why don't you try yours on to make sure it's right? I always worry when they're so quick to get them to us."

I unbuttoned my uniform shirt and laid it on the counter. She helped me put my head through the top between two stretchy pieces of fabric and then pulled elastic strips around my body from the back to Velcro to the front. It was heavier than I thought it would be.

"Okay twist your body."

I twisted side to side.

"Now sit down," she said offering me a chair.

I did.

"Does everything feel okay? Nothing pinches?"

"Other than being heavy, it's perfect," I said.

"Might as well keep it on since you'll be wearing it every day from now on," she said handing me my shirt.

I put it back on. Thankfully it still buttoned with the extra bulk.

"You don't even need bigger shirts." Michelle smiled. "Make sure you have that other girl try hers on within the next week so we can get it changed if it doesn't work. Have her twist and sit like I did with you."

I agreed.

"Oh Lord help me," Michelle said looking over my shoulder.

I turned to see what she was looking at. Hal Ward was walking toward us, his gaze locked on Michelle.

"Hello Officer Ward," Michelle said, her voice a bit saltier than it had been with me. "What can I do for you?"

"I'm here to pick up my gun." He didn't even acknowledge that I was standing there.

"I'm afraid it still isn't here. I told you I'd call you the moment it came in," she said.

Hal looked like he was about to explode. "It has been too long. This is ridiculous. I'd like to speak to a supervisor."

Michelle looked almost relieved to pass him off onto someone else. "I'll get him."

Hal turned and finally noticed my presence. "Don't I know you from somewhere?" He looked at my badge. "Ah, yes. You're Nikki's little friend."

He really was an ass.

"How are you doing?" I asked trying to be considerate.

"I'm fine." He huffed.

"I hear Jordan is doing better," I lied.

His face barely changed. "Where'd you hear that?"

"At the hospital. Have you been there lately?"

"I'm a busy man. I have work," he said.

"And you're mad at Alex for wanting to quit football aren't you?" I pushed.

His eyes narrowed. "Who told you he wanted to quit?"

"Doesn't matter," I said keeping my voice calm, chipper even.

He watched me for a moment. "Of course I'd be upset if he wanted to quit."

"Mad enough you'd hurt his best friend to make sure he played?"

Hal lunged forward, his hands reaching for my shoulders.

"Officer Ward." Michelle's voice stopped him in his tracks. "What exactly do you think you're doing?"

"You need to ask her that." He sounded like a petulant child. "She's accusing me of hurting my son's friend."

"Well, did you?" Michelle asked.

"Of course I didn't. I don't have to take this." He turned and stomped away.

"Thanks for getting rid of him for me," Michelle said. "Do you really think he hurt someone?"

"He's number one on my suspect list," I said.

"I didn't know park rangers did that kind of work."

"We don't." I smiled. "Have a good day. Thanks for your help."

"Anytime," Michelle said. "And I think he could do it too, if you want my opinion on it."

"Thanks." I smiled. He absolutely could have done it, and his reaction to my questions made me suspect him all the more.

I got a text message from Luke before I got back to the reservoir.

You went too far this time

I have no idea what you're talking about.

Two words. Hal. Ward.

No clue.

Watch your six.

His last text sent a chill down my spine. Hal had already reported me, and I'd only asked a couple of questions. If that wasn't suspicious, I didn't know what was.

The rest of the shift was so boring I almost fell asleep in my truck. Reginald and his tiny dog tucked up in his coat went to their usual ice fishing spot, and Dave was back in the cove.

From what I could tell, the fish weren't biting.

Antonio left sometime while I was picking up my vest. Whatever. I was tired of caring. If he wanted to ignore me, so be it.

Just as I was closing the main gate and sliding back into Cherry Anne's driver seat, my phone buzzed.

Nikki.

Alex is waking up.

I'll be right there.

I hit the gas. Alex could tell us everything.

"He's still groggy and not talking, but his eyes are open," Nikki said when I walked into the room.

"Alex, this is Rylie. She works with me. She's the one who found you," Nikki said.

Alex gave me a small smile. Henry was cuddled up on the bed next to his big brother, fast asleep.

"Now girls, don't overwhelm him," Elaine said from Alex's bedside. "I know you want to know what happened, but his health is what matters most right now."

"How's Jordan?" I whispered to Nikki.

"Bad," Nikki turned away from Alex. "He's not making any progress."

"If he dies, does this turn into a murder investigation?" I asked.

Nikki shrugged. "If they think someone left him out there to die, I suppose so."

"Water?" Alex's voice sounded like sandpaper grinding over a rough piece of wood.

Elaine held up the hospital-issued water jug, and he sipped from the straw.

"Alex, what happened to you?" Nikki asked.

Elaine looked like she might stop Nikki, but Alex smiled at his cousin. Their bond was unmistakable.

"Stupid. I was stupid." He turned to his mom. "I'm so sorry. Dad—"

"Shhh. It's okay. Dad will be here when he gets off his shift."

Alex nodded but didn't look satisfied with that answer. Was Elaine trying to cover for Hal? Was Alex about to tell us something incriminating about his father?

"I know you're exhausted, but can you tell us about that night?" Nikki pressed.

"There was a party." His voice was quiet, but the color in his cheeks had returned some. "I drank." He turned to Elaine. "Sorry, Mom."

She squeezed his hand but said nothing.

"I broke up with Debbie."

"Why?" Nikki asked. "You two had been together forever."

"She didn't get me anymore. We were headed in two different directions." He sighed and laid his head back on his pillow.

"What is she doing here," Hal's angry voice came from behind us.

Nikki turned to face her uncle. "Who?"

"This trouble-maker," he pointed his finger inches from my nose.

"I only asked you a couple of questions," I said. "I wasn't trying to cause trouble."

"You're a *park ranger*, not an investigator. You have no right to ask me anything."

"Stop, Dad," Alex whispered from the bed.

Hal's face transformed from anger to caring father. "You're awake?" He wrapped Alex up in his arms, waking Henry. "You're awake!"

"I should probably go," I said while Hal didn't have me in his crosshairs.

"I'll go with you," Nikki said. "Bye Alex. I'll be back tomorrow." She bent down next to her uncle and kissed Alex on his forehead. "I'm so glad you're okay."

"Bye cuz," Alex said with a smile.

The parking lot was nearly empty when we got down to our cars.

"What was Uncle Hal talking about?" Nikki asked.

I had to tell her. "I think he may have been the one who hurt Jordan."

I braced myself for her to hit me, either with her hand or her words. But no slap came.

"He may have," she said after a pause.

"I asked him about it at Hentemens when I was picking up our vests. You need to try yours on, by the way."

She nodded. "You're freaking crazy. My uncle could ruin your life."

"Let him try," I said keeping the fear I felt from my voice. "I think he's using intimidation to keep me from the truth."

"What can we do?"

"We could search his house, his car, whatever. See if we can find Jordan's clothes."

"That's an option. We just have to be careful and not disturb anything. Luke would kill us if we messed up the crime scene," she said.

"We'll be careful," I said.

"How was your shift?" Garrett asked when I'd finally made it to his place.

"Fine. Nothing huge happened. But Alex woke up. That's why I'm so late."

He nodded but didn't look thrilled.

"What's wrong?" I asked.

"I just worry about you," he said. "I thought you'd be home earlier."

"I went to the hospital," I said. "To talk to Alex."

"Do you think maybe you should go to police academy?" he asked. "You seem more interested in solving crimes than being a park ranger."

I instantly got defensive. "I don't want to be a cop. I love being a park ranger."

"Then stop investigating crimes that the police should be handling."

"It's Nikki's cousin. I'm trying to help her."

"You don't even like Nikki. For the longest time all you could talk about was how awful she was."

"Things change. This is who I am." I tried to keep my voice down but failed. "And if I wasn't this person, you might be in prison right now."

"I had already told the cops about Derrick. They were narrowing in on him. All you did was almost get yourself and my mother killed."

Really? That's what he thought about me?

"I'll see you later. I'm going to my parent's house. Come on Fizzy."

Fizzy reluctantly left Babbitt's side and followed me out the door.

Part of me thought Garrett might follow me out, but I wasn't terribly surprised when he didn't.

Coffee with Marlene, Eli Hudson's mom, was a weekly treat I hadn't missed once since I'd met her. Somehow this scrappy little fireball clothed like royalty had become one of my best friends.

As I sat on an oversized leather chair, Marlene handed me a cup of coffee—exactly how I liked it—from her enormous stainless steel coffee pot.

"What's the weekly dirt?" she asked like she did every week.

"I've been looking for an apartment. I think I'm going to move in with Shayla."

"Not Garrett?" she asked.

"I don't think we're quite ready for that." We still hadn't made up from last night's argument. He had texted that he was sorry and I responded that I was too, but I was still irritated. "We got in our first fight last night."

"And how did that go?"

"Like any other fight, I guess. He told me I should be a cop with all of the investigating I'm doing."

She sat forward. "What are you investigating now?"

"It's nothing, really. You probably heard about the two boys from North-Central High School?"

"The football players?" she asked. "Alex and—"

"Jordan," I said. "They were best friends, and somehow both of them almost ended up dead the same night."

"Was there a girl involved?"

"Sort of. But I don't exactly know how." Why did everyone immediately go to it being a girl's fault?

"Drugs?"

"Alex had some in his system," I said. "How did you know?"

"There's almost always drugs when it comes to these things."

These things. I almost laughed. This woman knew more about crime from living in what she called the hood than I could ever learn. She'd lived a very full and exciting —if not somewhat dangerous—life.

"But he wasn't a normal drug user," I said. "In fact, everyone who knows him swears up and down he had never taken drugs in his life."

"Maybe someone gave it to him."

"Okay, but why?"

"That's a good question." She smiled and took another sip. "You're smart, you'll figure it out."

I shook my head. I wasn't sure.

"Eli played well last week," I said changing the subject. Eli was her gorgeous Denver Bronco Quarterback son.

"He needs to run the ball more. He's going to wear out his arm throwing so much."

She was so proud yet so critical of Eli. But when he was around, she turned into a ball of goo. He had that effect on women.

"This boy, Alex, sounds like he would have eventually played in the NFL," she said.

"From what I hear he was the star of the team," I said. "But between you and me, he didn't want to play anymore."

"That changes everything. You can't make a teenage boy do anything he doesn't want to do."

"Did Eli ever want to quit?" I asked.

"Never. Football is in his blood. Has been since he was a baby." She beamed with pride. "You should talk to his coach. Coaches seem to know about these things."

I thought about Nikki's high school sweetheart. Maybe I could get some answers out of him.

We sat quietly for a moment sipping the delicious coffee and looking out the windows over a trail system in a valley that meandered between rows of houses on either side.

"Did you say you found an apartment?" Marlene asked.

"Shayla started looking. The only one I found was a studio for two thousand dollars on the bad side of town."

"Typical. You know, I own a couple of apartment complexes, I could cut you a deal."

"Really?"

"Of course. Just say the word."

"Thank you so much. I'll talk to Shayla about it."

She smiled.

My phone lit up with the number I'd almost forgotten.

Meet me in an hour. Same place as last time. Come alone.

I looked at the time. I'd have to let Nikki know I might be late meeting her.

Ok.

18

The bartender remembered my order and handed me a beer when I approached the bar. "Trying again, huh?" he said with a bit of condescension.

"It's not what you think," I began, but he looked like he neither believed me nor cared. "Whatever." I handed him the money and took my beer to a booth in the back facing the door.

I was early by five minutes, and at precisely an hour after the text, the door to the bar opened, and a man I'd only seen in photographs walked in.

Hal Junior, Alex's brother, was dressed in khaki pants, a black button-down shirt, and a black tie.

"You're the one who's been texting me?"

He sat down across from me. "Did you expect someone else?"

"I didn't expect anyone. How did you get my number?"

"I have my ways," he said with a smug smile.

I was a bit unnerved that he'd gotten my personal cell

phone number, but I could always change it after this was resolved. "What do you have to tell me?"

"This wasn't an accident."

"What wasn't an accident?" I asked.

He leaned in closer. "Alex. Jordan. It was all orchestrated."

"Why tell me, not the cops?"

"Nikki trusts you. The cops are all idiots around here."

"Isn't your dad a cop?" I asked.

He frowned. "Yeah."

"Okay." That was a box I had no interest in unpacking. "Then tell me why you think this wasn't an accident."

Hal looked around to make sure the bartender wasn't listening before he leaned forward and whispered, "He had drugs in his system. My brother never did drugs."

That was it? "I already knew that." I shook my head.

I should have known better. Of course, this was going to be a dead end.

"But it's proof that someone drugged him."

"No, it's proof that he took drugs. And even if someone drugged him, did they tie him to the snowmobile and make him crash into that tree?" I knew I was being patronizing, but I couldn't help it. This guy was wasting my time.

"It was my dad," he blurted out.

Now we were getting somewhere. "Your dad? As in the cop?" Even though I'd had the same thought, I didn't want to let on. I wanted to make him work for it a little bit.

"He and Alex had a big fight that night about playing football. Alex didn't want to play anymore."

I nodded.

"I think he drugged Alex to try and get him to stay home so he could take out Jordan. Without Jordan, Alex would have to play."

I almost brought up the fact that their dad would almost certainly know about the drug-testing rule. And that the cups from the party tested positive for the drug Alex had ingested.

But, the image of Alex's dad screaming in my face kept popping into my mind. Maybe he'd had a lapse of judgment. He could have gone to the party. And the coach probably would have turned the other cheek especially with the championship game coming up.

"Let me make sure I understand. You think when your dad and Alex had their argument, your dad drugged Alex to get him to stay home?"

Hal nodded.

"Then he found Jordan, took off his clothes, and left him in a locked reservoir on the beach to die?"

"He has master keys for all the locks in the city. How else would Jordan have ended up almost naked on that beach?"

I shrugged.

"But then Alex didn't stay home. He took the snow-mobile—probably because he wasn't in his right mind—and went on a nighttime ride." Hal looked more irritated than worried.

"Yeah that one really backfired on my dad," he said looking at the door as an old biker guy walked in and took a seat at the bar.

"You weren't a football player were you?" I asked.

He shook his head. "Much to my father's disappointment. It was always Alex this and Alex that. Alex is such a team player blah, blah, blah. But Alex took all the glory for himself, and everyone knew it."

"Okay, so any other suspects?" I asked.

"I guess the coach could have done it," he said. "But I'm almost one hundred percent sure it was my dad."

"Where were you the night Alex fell through the ice?" I asked.

Hal's face turned almost purple. "I was in my dorm room."

"And where do you go to college?"

"Mining College."

"Not too far from the reservoir." I leaned forward. "Do you have someone who can verify that you were in your dorm?"

Hal's eyes darted around. "You can't possibly think I did this?"

"You seem to have some serious jealousy issues when it comes to Alex."

"Why? Because I had to work for everything I've gotten? Because I wasn't handed scholarships and perfect grades for playing a stupid game? Because my father practically ignored me my entire life because I couldn't throw a stupid oblong ball?"

He looked mad enough to throw the table. Thankfully, it was bolted to the floor. "Yeah, that sounds about right."

"I didn't do this. I wouldn't hurt anyone. Especially not my brother."

"Maybe it was an accident. Have you ever taken drugs before? Maybe you wanted to show Alex the ropes. Give him a high after your dad got angry about him not wanting to play football."

"I have never done drugs. I would never." He stood. "You're insane. I should have never met you here."

Both of our phones buzzed. He raised an eyebrow.

I checked mine.

Come quick. Alex's not doing well.

Hal must have gotten Nikki's text as well. His face drained of color.

He didn't even look back at me before practically running out of the bar.

"He may be a nerd, but at least this one showed up," the bartender said as I made my way out. "You can do better if you ask me."

My mind was so focused on Alex, I couldn't even come up with a good comeback.

Cherry Anne sped as fast as her rear-wheel drive wheels would carry her on the icy roads. Thankfully, I'd practiced doing donuts in the high school parking lot growing up, so I knew how to handle a bit of slippage.

When I arrived at the hospital, Nikki stood in the hallway crying on her mother's shoulder.

"Nikki, is he okay? What happened?"

She wrapped her arms around my neck and melted into me, her tears soaking through my coat. The smell of peppermint in her hair told me she and Luke were still together and that she had used his shampoo recently. "He's gone."

The slight twinge of jealousy was replaced with extreme sadness for my sorta-friend. "I'm so sorry."

"He was doing so well." She sobbed. "And then he crashed."

"The doctor said it was cardiac arrest from the stress his body went through," Nikki's mom said, tears welling in her eyes too.

"Cardiac arrest, my ass," Nikki said pulling away from me. "This wasn't an accident. None of this was."

Her mom and I stood in shock staring at Nikki.

"Someone wanted him dead." She brushed the tears from her cheeks. "And now he is."

No one spoke. I was trying to make sense of it all.

Someone had drugged Alex at the party. But he had willingly taken the snowmobile and crashed it. No matter which way I twisted it, I couldn't pin this one on murder.

Marlene was right. I needed to talk to his coach.

"Nikki, if you want to say your goodbyes, you should do it now," her dad said.

She stood up to her full height, at least two inches taller than me in her heels, wiped the tears from her eyes and walked into the room.

Hal, Elaine, and Alex's two brothers walked out of the room like zombies. Hal Senior had his arm around Elaine as she cried into his chest.

Before Hal could order me to leave, I walked away.

I wanted to go home and hug my sister, to hug my mom and dad, to hug Shayla and Garrett and. . .

Luke was walking toward me.

He wrapped me in a hug and tears sprung to my eyes. There was the peppermint smell. They'd probably showered together. Yuck.

I let go of the hug and smiled as sincerely as I could. "Nikki's in with him right now, but I'm sure she'll be happy to see you."

"Are you okay?"

Was I? "Yeah. I just feel bad for Nikki and their family."

"If you need anything, you can always call me."

"Unless you're in another country."

Luke frowned. "Do you want me to stay?"

My heart did a flip-flop. This was not a matter in which I should have a say. "I don't know. It's your call. I'm sorry, I shouldn't have said that."

I turned to walk away, but he grabbed my hand.

"We *can* be friends, you know?"

I didn't know if that was possible, but I nodded. "I know."

"Luke, I'm so glad you're here," Nikki's mom said from behind me.

Before he could stop me again, I turned and walked away with tears running off my chin. My makeup was probably completely smeared.

I ducked into a bathroom and took a look in the mirror. It wasn't as bad as I'd thought. I ran a scratchy brown paper towel under my eyes and took a breath to steady my emotions.

The door flung open slamming against the cinderblock wall.

"What were you doing in his room?" a girl's voice snarled.

I ducked into a stall as quickly as I could and stood on the toilet seat so they wouldn't see my legs.

"I just wanted to see him, that's all," another girl's voice—scared and small—said.

"Did you think I wouldn't know about the two of you? Of course, I knew. Alex and I had been together for years."

The other girl whimpered.

"And then I find you in his room before he goes into a sudden cardiac arrest." I finally placed the snarly voice—Debbie. "What did you do to him?"

"I didn't do anything—I would never hurt Alex. I lo—"

The sound of flesh against flesh cut off her words. Debbie had just slapped the girl. I tried to peek through the crack in the door, but I couldn't see anything.

"Don't tell me you loved him. *I* loved him and look what he did to me."

"Did you do this?" the small voice asked. "Did you kill him?"

She took another slap in the face for that one.

"Do I look like a murderer to you?" Debbie's voice echoed off the tile and concrete. "Do I?"

My guess was she did look like a murderer at that moment. I couldn't take it anymore. Debbie needed to be stopped.

I opened the door of the stall. "What the hell do you think you're doing?" I said with as much command in my voice as I could muster.

Debbie let go of the girl's shirt. She was the same girl

I'd seen sneaking out of Alex's room before. The one with the silver Jetta.

"We were just having a little chat," Debbie said.

The girl took the opportunity to run out of the bathroom. I wanted to chase after her, but I needed to talk to Debbie more.

"You look like a murderer to me," I said. "I mean, if you want an honest answer. She surely wasn't going to give you one."

Debbie looked like she might try and slap me, but that would be a mistake. I'd had my fair share of knock down, drag outs with my sister, Megan.

"I didn't hurt Alex," she said through gritted teeth.

"Then who did?" I took a step toward her so she had to look up to see my eyes. "Who gave him the drugs?"

Her eyes darted to the side. She was trying to come up with a lie. Which meant she knew something.

"I don't know. It wasn't me though." She shuffled backward.

"Do you think someone really killed him?" I asked. "Or were you just mad that a girl with mousy brown hair and glasses could take your varsity football player boyfriend from you?"

"She didn't take him from me. He was just confused," Debbie said. "He would have come back."

"He was starting a new life, wasn't he? He was going to quit football, give up his scholarships, find a new girl."

She looked down at her Ugg boots.

"Sounds like a pretty good reason to hurt someone," I said.

"I didn't hurt him," she said. "But someone did."

"Who?" I was getting close. "Was it his brother? His dad? Jordan? The coach?"

Her expression didn't change at the mention of any of their names.

She put her hands on her hips. "Wouldn't you like to know?"

Ugh. I hated mean girls.

"You're not a cop. Just a lowly park pig." She narrowed her eyes. "Oink."

The only thing saving her from a slap across that ugly-pretty face was the fact that I was an adult, and I was certain she would press assault charges.

"Now if you'll excuse me, I have cheerleading practice to get to." She turned and walked out.

19

I arrived at the school just in time for football practice to begin. The team was warming up running drills down the field. The cheerleaders were outside practicing too. Debbie was at the top of the pyramid dressed in red and black sweats, hat, and gloves.

The coach stood on the sidelines with his arms crossed over his chest.

"Hi Brody, my name is Rylie Cooper. We met at the hospital."

His face flashed with irritation. "Okay."

"Your team looks a little—uh—small," I said. There didn't seem to be enough of them to play a game let alone the state championship.

"The captain of the team just died. His backup is in the hospital knocking at death's door too," Brody said without looking at me. "Would you want to be at football practice?"

"Why didn't you cancel practice?" I asked. "I didn't

think you were going to be able to play in the championship game since you don't have a quarterback."

"We will be playing. Regardless of who dies."

Harsh.

The assistant coaches were yelling at the boys to run faster, harder.

"How are you doing?" I pushed. "It's gotta be hard losing your best players."

His eye twitched. "Best *players*? Alex was our best player. But he was more than that. He was a good kid. Someone the younger kids looked up to. He had a bright future ahead of him."

"In football?" I pushed.

He glanced at me and then back at the field. "In whatever he wanted to do."

"You knew he didn't want to play football anymore."

Brody exhaled, his breath visible against the darkening sky. "Of course I knew. I was his coach."

"What about Jordan? You insinuated he wasn't your best player."

"That's because he wasn't. Not by a long shot. He rode Alex's coattails. But I'd kill to have him here now, especially since Alex's not coming back." His voice was gravelly with emotion.

"Well, it looks like someone may have killed to make sure Alex wouldn't come back."

His eyes narrowed. "I thought he had a heart attack."

"Maybe. Maybe not." I shrugged. "Do you know anyone who might want to kill Alex?"

"Jordan," he said quickly. "But we all know he couldn't have done it."

"But Jordan was his best friend."

"Like I said, he rode Alex's coattails. He was just waiting for Alex to mess up so he could take the lead."

"Do you think Jordan could have drugged Alex at that party?"

"I'd be surprised if it wasn't him. It makes the most sense. If Alex got a positive drug test, he wouldn't be able to play. Jordan would be up next."

It did make the most sense.

"Do you have a theory on what happened to Jordan?" I asked.

He shook his head. "Jordan probably got drunk, stripped down, and decided to go running on the beach. I wouldn't have put it past him."

"I found him. He was naked except for his boxers. And his clothes were gone. The park was locked, and the beach is at least a mile from the nearest walk-in gate. We didn't find any cars parked at any gates. It was below zero that night. How do you explain that?"

"I don't have to explain anything. What's done is done. If something happened, the police should investigate."

They were. But so was I. And I knew I was getting close.

"Thank you for your time."

Debbie watched me as I walked back across the field and between the stands toward the parking lot.

"Psst," someone said from beneath the bleachers.

I twisted toward the sound. "Yeah?"

The mousy-haired girl with glasses took a step into the light. "I need to talk to you." Her cheek was red where

Debbie had slapped her, her eyes swollen—probably from crying.

I walked under the bleachers.

"I was with Alex the night he—"

"The night he was in the accident?" I asked.

She nodded.

"You were at the party?"

"I'm not invited to those parties. But he came to my house after he and his dad got into an argument."

"Before he took the snowmobile," I said.

"He didn't hurt Jordan."

"I didn't figure he did."

"But that's what everyone thinks. And now he's going to be remembered for murdering someone instead of—" she sobbed. "Of how amazing he was."

I patted her on the back. "It's okay. I'm going to figure this out."

She pushed her glasses up on her nose.

"Is there anything else you can tell me about that night?"

"Alex was upset when he showed up at my window. My bedroom is in the basement—"

I nodded. Alex had snuck in.

"He said his dad was going to disown him. He told him he didn't want to play football anymore. That he was going to go to college with me."

"So his dad was mad, and Alex was upset."

"But it was more than that. He was so out of it. He was talking nonsense and stumbling all around. He told me he finally broke up with Debbie. She obviously took it badly. He wanted us to run away that night. We haven't even graduated."

"You said no."

Tears streamed down her cheeks. "It's my fault he got on that snowmobile. My fault. I should have stopped him."

I grabbed both of her shoulders. "Listen to me," I said. "This is not your fault. You were being sensible. Alex had been drugged."

"I should have been able to tell."

"Have you ever done drugs?"

She shook her head.

"Been around anyone doing drugs?"

"No."

"Then how would you have known he was under the influence? He obviously drank regularly. And he was upset. Stop blaming yourself. The person to blame is whoever put drugs in his drink."

She nodded. "But who did that?"

"I don't know yet. But I have an idea," I said not wanting to show too much of my hand.

"I think it was Debbie. She's pure evil. She used to torture Alex."

"As in physically torture?" I asked.

"Physically, emotionally, mentally. It took Alex forever to finally stand up to her. And once he did, she lost it."

I was convinced it was Jordan. But Debbie was looking more and more like she might be responsible for Alex's drug intake.

"Why would she give him drugs?"

"To get him kicked off the team. She had no idea how little football meant to him. No one did."

"Except you."

She stared off into the darkness behind me. "Except me."

20

"I think I found a place for us," Shayla said when we met for a drink Monday night. "It's on the outskirts of Prairie City—close for both of us once I get the job on PCPD."

"Sounds perfect. Is it relatively inexpensive?"

"Only $500 a month per person. We would each have a bedroom, but we'd have to share a bathroom."

"What's the catch? It seems too good to be true."

This was significantly less expensive than the studio apartment.

"It's not in the best area of town, that's all. But we'll be okay." She didn't make eye contact when she said this.

"Shayla?"

"Okay, it's in a terrible part of town. But I'll have a gun and you have pepper spray and it'll be fine. We only have to sleep there."

"I think I may have found a better option," I said remembering what Marlene had offered. "Marlene owns several apartment buildings. She said she would be willing to give us a deal."

"Really?" Shayla looked like she might hug me. "It's just that there is nothing in our price range. It's nuts. I can keep looking, but this is the best I've found."

"It's no problem. Let's go look at the place Marlene has, and then we can make a decision."

"Do you think that'll be a conflict of interest or anything?" Shayla asked.

I thought about it for a minute. "We're responsible, we'll pay rent on time and take care of the apartment. I don't think it'll be a problem."

"And maybe her studly son will make an appearance every once in a while?" Shayla wiggled her eyebrows up and down.

"Shayla!" I laughed. "We're both in relationships."

"Doesn't mean we can't look every now and then."

I shook my head. Looking is exactly what got you into trouble. First it's innocent looking, then it turns into flirting, then it turns into kissing . . .

Nope. Not good.

"Are you sure you don't want to move in with Garrett?"

"I'm sure. We're not exactly talking right now." I fiddled with my phone. "I mean, we've texted a little bit, but . . ."

"What happened?" she asked.

"He got all protective and worried about me investigating these crimes. And then he said that I was basically just making a fool of myself because the cops can handle it and they don't need my help."

Shayla took a sip of her beer. "He's right. About the cop thing," she said slowly. "Partially, at least."

My blood pressure was rising. Of course she would say that. She was almost a cop herself.

"But you're not making a fool of yourself. Your instincts are on point. Even if Luke hasn't said it, you've been incredibly helpful with the last two cases."

I felt bad for getting angry.

"The first fight is hard, but you have to dust yourself off and work through it. Especially if you love each other."

We did, right? I mean, we'd said it and everything.

"You're right. I should talk to him."

Shayla smiled.

"But even so, I'm not moving in with him."

"Eventually you will, though." She pushed her curly blonde hair behind her. "Like when he proposes or when you're married or—"

"Whoa. Slow down there. What makes you think he's going to propose? We've only just said we love each other." Just the thought made my heart pound against my ribs.

"At your age, that's the natural progression of things."

"At my age? I'm only a few years older than you."

"Yeah and Garrett's a few years older than you. He's definitely at that age."

Oh my goodness. She was right.

"Are you okay? You look like you might puke."

"It's just—I'm not ready to get married."

"Weren't you engaged to your last boyfriend?" Shayla asked. "Maybe it's just that you're not ready to get married to *Garrett*."

He couldn't possibly be ready to propose. We'd only been together a few months. That wasn't nearly enough time to decide you wanted to marry someone.

"Let's talk about something else. Something less scary like murderers."

"Murderers?" Shayla shook her head and took a drink of her beer.

"Alex died."

"Of a heart attack," Shayla said.

"I don't know, Shay. It seems awfully convenient. Yesterday he was talking, smiling. And today he has a heart attack? He's a teenager."

"Who went through a terrible accident. His body may not have been able to withstand supporting itself."

"If, hypothetically, I found out who put the drugs in his drink, would they be charged with murder?" I asked.

"Hypothetically?" She raised her eyebrows. "What do you know?"

"Nothing concrete yet. But I'm getting close, I can feel it."

"They probably wouldn't get charged with murder, but maybe involuntary manslaughter. Have you told Luke about this?"

"He's got his hands full with Nikki. Plus this time, it's not dangerous. They're just a bunch of teenage kids."

"Still, be careful," Shayla said. "You never know what someone might do."

"I'll talk to Marlene and see when we can go visit the apartment," I said.

"Perfect, I can't wait to get out from under my mom's thumb."

A few weeks ago, I would have said the same thing, but part of me might actually miss my mom's antics.

———

Sitting in my car, I stared down at my phone and the text message I'd typed out.

I need your help.

I knew the moment I pushed send Luke would put on his cape and come running. It was just the kind of guy he was. I also knew it would take him away from Nikki in her time of need.

I deleted the message and shut off my phone. It wasn't that late, but they could be in bed.

I pulled out my phone again.

Can we talk?

I hit send before I could second guess myself.

                                   Of course.

The message came back within seconds.

———

Garrett pulled me into a hug the minute I walked into the house. "I'm so sorry. I never should have said those things."

"And I'm sorry I didn't communicate I would be late that night. I didn't mean to make you worry. I'll do better in the future."

"I guess it's futile asking you to quit investigating these cases?"

I thought about that for a minute. "I don't think I could agree to stop."

He leaned in and kissed my forehead. "Can you agree to be careful?"

"I'll do my best," I said. "Now, how about I make dinner?"

He pulled back. "Are you sure you're the Rylie I'm dating?"

"Oh hush." I pushed his shoulder. "I make a mean spaghetti."

When I'd offered to make spaghetti, I hadn't considered how hard it would be to keep his kitchen in pristine condition while cooking something that was bound and determined to make a mess. It took almost an hour to make it and clean as I went.

"This looks amazing," Garrett said when I set his plate down in front of him.

"Sorry it took so long."

"It's okay. I like eating dinner at ten o'clock at night." He laughed.

"I think Shayla and I may have found an apartment," I said after I sat down and began to eat.

"You know, the offer still stands for you to move in

here." He took a sip of the red wine he'd picked for dinner. "Then you could save money."

It was so tempting to just give in and agree to move in with him. Then I remembered how hard it was to cook dinner in such a spotless kitchen.

"What is going through your head right now?" he asked.

"Nothing." I couldn't tell him that his house was too clean. Then he'd think I was a slob.

"Just tell me. I can see there's something on your mind every time I bring up living together." He smiled as if everything in the world was just peachy and perfect and I was the most beautiful girl in the world.

"Your house is just so . . ."

"So what?" He looked around trying to find clues as to what I was talking about.

"So clean. Not that I can't be clean. I can. Obviously. I made dinner without making a mess at all. But your house is overly clean. It's—"

"Rylie, stop." Garrett laughed. "My house is clean because I have a housekeeper. Haven't you met her?"

The only person I'd met claiming to be a housekeeper had been a woman who wanted to kill me.

I slowly shook my head.

"That's probably because she comes when we're working." He patted Babbitt on the head and fed him a meatball. "Trust me, I am not the neat freak I seem to be."

My head spun. Did this mean I should move in with him? That was really the only barrier. Or had it been an excuse?

"Is there another reason why we shouldn't live together? Formally, I mean?"

"We're not married," the words popped out of my mouth before I could swallow them down.

Garrett leaned back in his chair and eyed me with a small smile on his lips.

"Not that I'm saying we should get married. We only just said we loved each other. And it's too soon, right? It's too—"

"Rylie. Shhhh. It's okay. I know you weren't proposing." Garrett's smile was warm and fuzzy. It made me want to snuggle up next to him.

"Good. I'm glad. Because I really don't want to rush things."

"Moving in together would be a huge step."

"Very huge." I moved to sit in his lap. He wrapped his arms around me and kissed me so passionately it made my toes tingle.

21

Opening the reservoir on a snowy day was both the most boring thing and the most beautiful thing I could imagine. The ice shimmered as the sun rose. The sun peeked through the clouds as snow fell from the sky like nature's glitter.

I passed the time in the truck going over all of the possible scenarios that led to Alex's death.

Reginald tapped on my truck window forcing me from the investigation. He was pulling a sled with all of his fishing tackle, tent, and heater in it. "Were you sleeping?"

His little dog—Polly—popped her head out from the neck of his jacket.

"No, I wasn't sleeping," I said. "I was thinking."

"About what?" Reginald asked.

"Just all the stuff that's been going on with these football players."

He looked sad. "I heard one of them died."

"And the other one is holding on by a thread," I said. "I just wish I knew what happened."

"It was probably over some girl, if I had to guess. Teenage boys are only motivated by two things their stomachs and their—"

"I get the picture," I said stopping him.

"I went to North-Central High. I was a football player too. It's hit the whole town hard." He scratched his dog's head. "If I could help, I would."

"Thanks," I said. "Be careful out there. And keep Polly in your coat. Technically dogs aren't supposed to be out on the ice."

He rolled his eyes. "That's a dumb rule. Dogs weigh less than humans."

"It's not because of how much they weigh. They don't have the same reasoning skills. They might chase a bird onto thin ice and fall through."

"I'd save her if she did," he said.

"And that's exactly why we don't allow dogs on the ice." I laughed. "Because once the dog falls through, the owner goes after them. But dogs can usually get themselves out, whereas humans can't. So the dog survives and the human dies."

"Unless Super Ranger Rylie saves them," he said with a smile.

"Just keep her in your jacket."

Everyone let Reginald take his dog out with him. He had claimed it was an emotional support dog at some point and no one wanted to touch that.

"See you later," Reginald said.

Antonio's truck was in the ranger parking area when I closed up the plaza. I hadn't seen him all shift, but that seemed about right considering the last few weeks.

"Ranger Seven, Ranger Five."

"Go ahead," his voice came through the mic.

"I'm locking up the Plaza. Do you mind setting the alarm when you're done in the office?"

"Copy."

I couldn't help but roll my eyes. He could be so infuriating.

The gates were frozen, and I had to work at getting them closed. My hands were freezing. I couldn't have been more done with the day.

Heaven forbid Antonio help me close up.

No, he just sat in the office doing who knows what.

"Ranger Five, Ranger Seven?"

"Go ahead," I responded. I couldn't keep the irritation from my voice. Not that I'd tried.

"We have reports of someone in the water in the back of Marina Cove. You have the Gumby suits in your truck, right?"

"Affirm. I'll meet you there."

"Copy. Clear," he said.

I turned the truck around—nearly getting stuck in a snowdrift—and drove as fast as was safe back toward Marina Cove.

My heart pumped as quickly as the tires spun. I'd done many ice rescues between training and actual calls. I repeated the mantra—reach, throw, go—over and over in my head.

Antonio had gotten to the cove before me and stood

next to a giant heap of a man. Reginald waved his arms frantically when he saw my headlights. Antonio placed a hand on his back, but I don't know if Reginald even felt it.

I maneuvered the truck so the headlights shone on the cove, put it in park, and jumped out. "What happened?"

"You told me—" Reginald's voice was hysterical. "I never should have taken her."

He pointed to the lake.

"Who?" Antonio asked. He and I both strained to see where this person was. If they'd gone under, it would be much harder to get to them.

"Polly."

His dog.

"I should have gone in after her, but you said—"

"Where did she go in?" I asked.

Reginald pointed. "I don't see her."

"Do you want to go in or do you want me to?" I asked Antonio.

"You go in," he said. "I'll pull you out."

I was in the Gumby suit in less than two minutes. "Do you have a visual?"

Both men stared out onto the ice. The dog was tiny and white. Getting a visual was going to be nearly impossible.

"Zip me," I said to Antonio.

His hands shook, and he looked me in the eye for the first time in months. I gave him a small smile. "We got this."

He nodded and looked away.

"There," Reginald shouted. "She's right there."

Open water about thirty-five feet from shore held what looked like a splashing rat.

"The ice might not be stable getting out there," Antonio said. "I would approach from the right."

He clicked the carabineer to my suit.

"Reginald, you need to help Antonio pull me out once I get Polly, okay?"

Tears streamed down his face. It was amazing such a small animal could cause such a strong man so much pain.

"Good to go?" I asked Antonio.

"Yes."

I walked out onto the ice keeping my center of gravity low and my steps as wide as possible. Reach was an option. Throw, not so much. Go would probably be the outcome.

The ice crackled under my feet sending a chill up my legs. Polly's little legs swam as fast as they could.

"Come here, Polly," I called.

If she could rescue herself, it would be for the best.

She put her front paws onto the ice shelf but couldn't quite pull herself up.

"I'm coming," I said as reassuringly as possible.

The ice surrounding Polly was still thick. She had to have fallen in a man-made hole. Thank goodness it hadn't been Reginald.

I got on my hands and knees and reached a hand out toward her. She had gone back to swimming in the icy water and was impossible to catch.

"Going in," I yelled to Antonio.

I slid into the hole—big enough for at least three people—and pulled my arms and legs into a ball. Air rushed out of my suit, and Polly practically jumped into my arms.

I bobbed around trying to keep her above water while pushing myself into a position so I wouldn't crush her when Antonio pulled me out.

I put a hand on my head and then up in the air—the signal for Antonio to pull. The rope tightened, and I rolled to my side keeping the sweet little pup's shivering body cradled carefully in my arms.

Once I was on the ice shelf and Antonio stopped pulling, I stood and walked back to shore.

Reginald scooped Polly into his arms. "Oh baby, I'm so sorry. No more ice fishing for you."

She licked his face once.

"There's a towel in the back of my truck," I said. Antonio nodded and walked over to get it.

"Thank you so much, Rylie," Reginald said. "I'm sorry I didn't listen to you."

"I'm just glad you didn't go in after her." I smiled.

Antonio returned with the towel and Reginald wrapped Polly in it.

"Can you help me out of this suit?" I asked Antonio. Now that it wasn't a matter of life and death, it was awkward asking him to help me disrobe.

He undid the Velcro and pulled the zipper down far enough that I could pull the top half of the suit off.

On the path next to my truck, I heard clapping.

The three of us turned to see naked guy with a huge smile on his face. "That was seriously awesome," he said. "I wish I had my phone on me. But, alas, no pockets."

"Not again," Antonio mumbled under his breath. "Are you going to run if I try to catch you?"

Naked guy shrugged. "Maybe. Maybe not."

"Aren't you cold?" I asked trying not to look right at him.

"The cold air makes my pores practically non-existent," Naked guy said. "It's a rush better than drugs."

That reminded me of Alex. And Jordan. Had Jordan gone out there for the rush? I had to go see him. Guilt swelled through me. I hadn't visited him since the day he was taken to the hospital.

"I will give you a ride to your car," Antonio said. "The park is closed, and my shift was over twenty minutes ago."

Naked guy thought about this for a minute. "Okay."

They got into Antonio's truck, Antonio throwing a towel on the seat and saying something about covering up.

"Why don't I get you to your car too," I said to Reginald.

He was still snuggling Polly like a little baby doll. "Do you think she'll be okay?"

"I'd take her to the vet if I were you," I said. "But I think she'll be fine."

Polly wagged her tiny tail.

22

Jordan was still hooked up to all of the machines when I arrived early the next morning. No one else was in the room.

"Hey Jordan," I said quietly. "It's Rylie, the park ranger who found you."

I stepped a bit closer. His color had returned, and there were little bruises on his forehead. They were in a pattern.

"Hello?" A voice from behind me almost made me scream.

"Hi," I said. It was Jordan's mom. "I'm Rylie, the park—"

"I remember you." She smiled.

"Any word on how he's doing?" I asked.

"He's still not breathing on his own." She looked too exhausted to cry.

My heart sank. Were both of these boys going to die?

"Do you know what those bruises are on his head?" I asked. "I didn't see them when I found him."

"They didn't show up until he got his color back."

"It looks like some sort of pattern," I said. "Little stars maybe?"

She looked closer and shrugged. "Perhaps."

"Do you have any idea how this could have happened?" I asked as gently as I could.

She slumped down into the chair next to Jordan's bed and grabbed his hand. "I've been over and over it in my mind. Jordan never would have done something like this alone. I think it was Alex. I guess now we'll never know."

"It wasn't Alex. I know that for certain." Well as certain as the word of a teenage girl.

She narrowed her eyes at me. "You're friends with his cousin. Of course you're going to defend him."

The last thing I wanted to do was cause her any additional heartache. "I'm sorry. I wasn't trying to defend anyone. I just wanted to know if you had any other ideas. If anyone has visited and acted weird or—well—anything."

She stared at Jordan's hand in hers.

"I'll just let myself out," I said turning toward the door.

"Debbie," she almost whispered.

"What?" I asked.

"Debbie has visited several times." She didn't look up when she spoke. "She never even liked Jordan."

"But Jordan liked her, didn't he?"

"He loved her," his mother corrected. "She could do no wrong in his eyes."

"Why would she do something like this?" I asked. "And how?"

"I don't know."

Nikki dropped her head into her hands. "I don't even want to go."

We were inside her uncle's house, searching every nook and cranny. She'd promised no one would be there—and they weren't . . . yet. If her uncle found us, not only would it start a civil war in their family, but I'd probably end up in jail. Just to be safe, my hair was up in a bun and I had on gloves to keep my fingerprints off everything.

"It's stupid," she said. "I know I should be there, but if I go, it's like I'm giving in to the fact that Alex's gone and he's never coming back. I don't know that I'm ready to accept that. Not yet."

"You'll have your mom and dad and Luke with you." I yanked open a drawer that held silverware and gently moved things around before closing it. What could he possibly be hiding in a silverware drawer?

My mind bounced back and forth between the task at hand and the information I'd gotten from Jordan's mom. I had to tell Nikki about it, but I didn't know how. Especially with the funeral coming up.

"Mom and Dad are both in helper mode, and Luke is off in his own world right now. I think it's the thought of possibly going to the Middle East. He just doesn't seem to care about me."

"Do you want me to go with you?" I asked.

Nikki's head jerked up. "You'd do that?"

Stupid.

Why couldn't I just keep my mouth shut? I hated funerals. They were the absolute worst.

"Of course I would."

"That would be amazing. Really, Rylie. Thank you."

"What time does it start?"

She gave me all the information. "But be there early so we can walk in together."

"I'm not family," I said.

"It doesn't matter."

We searched in silence for a few moments. She looked in closets, and I checked the kitchen cabinets.

"I went to see Jordan this morning," I said.

"How is he?" Nikki asked.

"Alive, but barely."

"I still think he did this to Alex."

"His mom thinks Alex did it to him," I said. "I told her he didn't."

"How can we know that, though? I mean, I know—knew—my cousin." She cleared her throat. "But he was on drugs, he could have done anything."

"Did you know he had a new girlfriend?"

"Alex or Jordan?"

"Alex. I met her the other night after I went to talk to your ex."

"You talked to Brody?" She stared at me. "Why?"

"Because I want to get to the bottom of this. It's really gotten under my skin."

"Tell me everything," she said.

I explained what Brody said about Jordan riding Alex's coattails and how Debbie had cornered the new girlfriend in the bathroom.

"What's the new girlfriend's name?" Nikki asked when my monologue had concluded.

"I never asked."

Nikki stood with her hands on her hips. "Let's go upstairs, to the bedroom. There's nothing down here."

"How will we know if we find Jordan's clothes?" I asked. "Won't they look just like Alex's? Or Henry's since he's smaller than Alex?"

"He wore the number fourteen. Their jersey number is printed on all of their school clothes," she said leading up the stairs. "You said you talked to Alex's new girlfriend, right?"

"After I talked to Brody, she pulled me under the bleachers at the school." We began methodically going through the rooms on the second floor. If only their house wasn't so large. "She told me Alex had gone to her house after his fight with his dad. He was there until he took the snowmobile."

"So he couldn't have hurt Jordan?"

"According to her." I shrugged. "And both she and Jordan's mom think Debbie has something to do with all of this. After the way Debbie acted in the bathroom, I would have to agree with them."

"What about Uncle Hal?" Nikki asked. "Do we still think he could have done it? Or are we searching for nothing?"

"I don't think we're searching for nothing. But I do think Debbie is a very real suspect too."

"But what did she do? Did she spike Alex's drink? There's no way she forced Jordan to take off his clothes and freeze to death."

"Maybe there is," I said. The gears in my brain spun so hard I was surprised steam wasn't coming out of my ears.

"If Jordan was drunk he would have done lots of stupid things, right?"

"Okay, I'll play along."

"Even his mom said he loved Debbie. So wouldn't he have followed her to the ends of the earth?"

"Probably."

"One of the kids I talked to said they saw Jordan and Debbie making out in a car at the party. What if she lured him to the beach? Acted all seductive and told him to take off his clothes?"

"And then?"

My brain hurt. He may have taken off his clothes but why would he have stayed there? All night? In the freezing cold?

"I don't know. But she took his clothes and left," I said.

"He would have chased after her."

"The theory needs some work," I admitted. "But it's plausible."

Nikki looked under her aunt and uncle's bed. "And you think she drugged Alex because he broke up with her?"

"Maybe," I said. "She's pretty crazy."

"Do you think she's the one who killed Alex in the hospital?"

"Maybe," I said slowly. "If someone did something to Alex in the hospital, it could have been her. But Jordan's mom seemed to have pretty negative feelings too."

She waved a hand as if she didn't care what I thought.

"Debbie always seemed so nice," Nikki said. "I guess it was all an act."

I hadn't seen Nikki so down . . . ever. Her usual edge was dulled by grief.

"We'll talk to her after the funeral. Together," Nikki said.

"Deal," I said. "There's nothing here. Your uncle is smarter than hiding anything in his house where his wife or Henry could find it."

She nodded. "I don't think we'll get access to his patrol car, but his personal truck is in the garage."

Why hadn't we started there? "Let's go."

There was nothing suspicious in the truck either. Nothing suspicious in the entire garage, in fact.

"It's a dead end," I said giving into defeat. "If he did it, we'll have to get him to confess. He's probably burned the evidence by now."

"You're right, I would have," Hal's voice echoed through the garage propelling me to my feet, my hands clasped into fists.

"Uncle Hal," Nikki said. "We were just—"

"I know exactly what you were doing." He had his arms crossed over his chest, his face full of shadows. "I just can't for the life of me figure out what made you think searching a police officer's home for clues was a good idea."

My knees shook. Every part of me was terrified of this man.

"We had to," I whispered so he wouldn't hear the fear in my voice.

"Had to?" He took a step toward both of us and moved his hands to his duty belt—his gun.

I swallowed. "Yes, sir." I figured being polite couldn't hurt. "We need to figure out who drugged Alex. Who tried to kill Jordan. And if that means we need to search for clues, then we will."

"Nikki. Do you agree with her?"

Nikki leveled her gaze at him. "Yes, Uncle Hal. And if you had anything to do with it, I'd like you to tell us."

"If I confess to you, what will you do with that information?" He looked from Nikki back to me. "Do you have a recorder going? Because even if I say something to you, it'll still be my word against yours in court."

I didn't have a recorder. I didn't have any way of proving it.

"Confessing to us is not the goal," I said. "We have no authority over the situation."

"You're absolutely right you don't." His pompous voice made me want to punch him.

"However, if you did something to one or both of those boys, and you confessed it to us, we would take that information to the police, and they would launch a full investigation." I was speaking out my ass. I had no idea if they would or not.

"I'm one of their most decorated officers," he said.

"And someone many people are afraid of," I added.

"But not you." He stepped closer to me, bending over slightly at the hips so he could look me right in the eye.

I didn't blink. "No. I'm not afraid of you." Okay, so I was, but I wouldn't give him the satisfaction of hearing those words come out of my mouth.

"I could shoot you for entering my house."

"You could," I said. "But would you shoot your own niece? The person Alex may have loved more than anyone else in the world?"

His gaze darted to Nikki then back to me. He stood back up to his full height towering over me. "You're good."

"I'm what?" My mind reeled.

The corners of his mouth twitched up slightly. "You'd make a damn good police officer."

Was he trying to change the subject? Get us away from some sort of evidence?

"I didn't do anything to Alex—" his voice caught on his son's name "—or Jordan. And I'm not trying to take your focus off the investigation. I have a solid alibi for that evening. I was working a case with several other police officers—many who despise me and would happily rat me out if I wasn't where I said I was."

Frustration swept over me.

"Uncle Hal, are you mad at me?" Nikki asked.

"Mad? Hell no. I'm proud. You stood up for what you thought was right. Anyone who can stand up to me is a tough SOB."

Nikki smiled a bit, the sadness not leaving her eyes.

"I need to thank you," he said to me.

"For what?"

"If you hadn't confronted me at Hentemens, I might never have gone to see Alex that night. My workaholic and avoidance tendencies are huge downfalls. And if I hadn't gone to see Alex, I might never have been able to make amends before—" he couldn't say the rest.

167

"I'm glad you were able to talk to him. I'm so sorry that he didn't make it."

"Don't be sorry, figure out what happened," he said. "I'm too close to the situation to see it clearly, but from what I've heard and what I've seen, I have every bit of confidence that if anyone can solve these cases, you can."

Nikki stood to the side with her mouth hanging open.

23

The only black dress I had was the one I wore when I went out on the town. Definitely not appropriate for a funeral. After I showered and did my hair and makeup the next day, I went to the mall to pick up something a bit more modest.

Of course, I had to show up at the mall just as the high school kids were getting out of class. I could hardly find parking, and once I did, I made my way through the crowd to a department store with reasonable prices. I couldn't blow my savings on a dress. Christmas was coming as was Cherry Anne's car payment. Plus, Marlene would charge us something to live in her building. I needed to be prepared.

I pulled four black dresses from the clearance rack and hurried to the dressing room. I only had about an hour before I had to be at the funeral if I wanted to get there when the family did and avoid Nikki's wrath.

The first dress made me look like I was from the 1800s and the second was too short. The third was a definite contender but had more lace than I was accustomed to. As I was pulling on the fourth dress, I heard someone crying in the dressing room next to me.

I almost asked if she was okay, but then I heard another voice.

"It's going to be okay, Deb. I know you miss him."

My ears perked up. Could it possibly be Debbie in the stall next to mine?

I leaned up against the wall closest trying to hear.

"I don't know why I care so much. He dumped me for that loser." Her sobs turned to soft hiccups.

"He was your boyfriend for a long time. You were a shoo-in for prom king and queen."

"Why couldn't it have been Jordan? He deserved it. Alex didn't."

"Don't say that," her friend hissed. "People will start thinking you had something to do with the Jordan incident."

I couldn't press my ear up against the wall any harder. Was she going to confess?

I should be recording the conversation. If talking to Hal taught me anything, it was that I needed to be more prepared. I fumbled for my phone.

"Well, I didn't," Debbie said.

Her friend was silent. My phone slipped from my hand and crashed onto the bench.

"Is someone over there?" Debbie called out.

I froze. The last thing I needed was more park pig jokes.

"Come on out," Debbie's voice was sweet and cold. "I

know you heard us talking." She pounded her fist on the door as if she was going to break it down.

I stayed silent. I wouldn't give her the satisfaction.

Eventually, she and her friend walked away. My watch told me I was running late. Nikki was going to kill me.

I looked at myself in the mirror. The fourth dress had cap sleeves, and the hem went down to my calves. The neckline didn't show any cleavage, but the fit accentuated my figure. The price was a bit much, even for the clearance rack. But it was the best choice.

I changed back into my jeans and hoodie and was leaving the room when I ran smack into Debbie.

Her bloodshot eyes widened with recognition. "I knew someone was in there."

"Hello, Debbie," I said with a smile.

"How much did you hear?" Debbie was gorgeous, but her outside appearance did not match her evil insides.

"Enough," I said. "It sounds to me like you know more than you're letting on. But don't worry, the police will figure everything out. They're *very* close to making an arrest."

Debbie's jaw dropped.

Before she could respond, I walked away.

Nikki stood next to Luke looking elegant as ever tapping her designer shoes on the concrete steps.

"It's about time you showed up." She yanked me by the arm into the church, Luke following behind with an I'm sorry look on his face.

We sat in the first row with the rest of the family. The church was the largest in the area with an auditorium feel. Huge photos of Alex in his football uniform, with Debbie at a school dance, and standing next to a brand new car with a big red bow on top were balanced on huge easels around a closed casket on the stage. Flowers various shades of red sat neatly around the photos and on top of the casket along with Alex's letterman jacket and a football.

Quiet sobs and hushed voices filled the air. I turned to watch as a group of high school kids walked in and sat in the back. Debbie locked eyes with me and glared.

What was she hiding? Had she hurt Jordan? Alex?

"What's going on with you?" Nikki asked beside me. I couldn't help notice her fingers entwined with Luke's, his thumb stroking hers.

"Nothing. I just hate funerals."

"What's to hate? The person's already dead." Nikki wiped a stray tear from her cheek.

"The smell," I said without thinking.

"The smell?" Nikki looked at me like I was sprouting another head.

"All funerals smell the same. Maybe it's the flowers or death or tears, but they smell."

Nikki inhaled. "I don't smell anything but your cheap perfume."

I bit my tongue. I wasn't even wearing perfume.

The service was the same as most funerals. I held it

together until Nikki spoke about when she and Alex were kids. She had the entire church in tears before she was finished.

"That was beautiful, what you said back there," I told her when we stood at the end of the family receiving line. "You could be a public speaker."

Nikki rolled her eyes. "Like you would know."

I only let her meanness go because I knew she was grieving and didn't mean it . . . probably.

"Hey Nikki," Brody said kissing her on the cheek.

Luke shot me a look.

"Can I chat with you for a minute?" He motioned to a more private area of the foyer.

Nikki smiled a real smile for the first time since Alex had died. "Of course."

He led her away from us, his hand dangerously close to her butt.

"I hate that guy," Luke muttered.

"He's her Luke," I said without thinking.

He looked at me with a confused expression. "Her what?"

"Uh—" I couldn't believe I had just said that out loud. "He's her high school sweetheart."

Luke nodded but, thankfully, didn't say anything else.

We watched as the two of them spoke with a familiarity that made me feel like we were watching an intimate moment. I averted my gaze.

"I'm sure it's nothing."

Luke looked at me. "Nothing. Sure." He nodded as if trying to convince himself. "How are you doing? I know you hate funerals."

"I haven't passed out yet." I thought of the time I'd fainted at the funeral of a victim we'd lost in a fire.

Luke rubbed my shoulder. "It was nice of you to be here with her. Even though she's not very nice to you."

"She's grieving."

We both looked to where she was laughing along with Brody as if she were at a party, not a funeral.

"Should I be worried?" Luke asked.

D ebbie tried to avoid Nikki and me after the funeral, but when she went to the bathroom, we took it as our opportunity to get her away from her friends.

"Hi Debbie," Nikki said when she emerged.

She jumped about two inches off the ground before her eyes met mine. "I don't want to talk to you. Either of you."

"We don't care if you don't want to talk to us. You're going to," Nikki said. "You're going to tell us exactly what happened with Alex."

"And Jordan," I added crossing my arms over my chest. My phone was strategically placed in my purse so it would hopefully record any possible admissions.

"You are insane. Both of you." She crossed her arms over her almost see-through gauzy black dress. "I don't know anything, and if you keep following me around trying to get me to talk or spying on me in dressing rooms, I'm going to call the police myself."

She turned to walk away, but Nikki grabbed her arm. "You listen to me you little shit, you're going to tell us everything. Everything." With gritted teeth and a red face, Nikki did look a little insane.

I touched Nikki's arm lightly, and she loosened her grip.

Debbie yanked her arm away and rubbed the spot Nikki had been holding.

"I know you know something. We're not saying you did it," I said. "But if you could tell us what happened, that would be good."

"Jordan put the drugs in Alex's drink," she said. "There. Are you happy?"

"Did you see him do it?" Nikki asked.

"No," Debbie said.

"Then how do you know?" Nikki asked.

Debbie's face paled. "It's the talk around school, you know?"

"Um, no," I jumped in. "You're lying. Try again."

Debbie shook her head. "I'm not lying. Everyone is talking about it. Jordan put drugs in Alex's drink so he would test positive and not be able to play in the championship game."

Nikki and I stood there for a minute.

"Can I go now? Or are you going to assault me again?"

"Is everything okay over here?" Luke appeared at my side.

"Everything is fine," I said. "Debbie was enlightening us about how Jordan put drugs in Alex's drink."

"Well, we can go ask him," Luke said. "He just woke up."

Excitement welled up inside me. "That's great," I said.

Debbie, however, did not look like she thought that was great. She turned on a heel and stomped away, the jewels on her handbag creating tiny reflections that followed her back to her group of friends.

25

Once Nikki had finished up with the funeral things. She, Luke, and I drove to the hospital in Luke's truck. I sat in the back while Nikki and Luke held hands in the front. The last time I'd been in his truck, I'd sat in the front seat holding Luke's hand.

I wrangled my thoughts back to the present. Jordan was awake. He was alive. But Alex had been too and then—

No.

I didn't want to think about that anymore. My eyes were all cried out from the funeral, and I was still a bit light-headed.

Jordan's parents stood in the hallway eagerly talking to the doctor. Where there was a worried frown on his mother's face the day before, there was now a happy smile.

When we walked into the room, Jordan was sitting up eating a cup of Jello.

"Hi Jordan," Luke said. "I'm Luke with Prairie City PD, I'm investigating your and Alex's cases. This is Rylie, she found you on the beach. And this is Nikki, she works with Rylie and is Alex's cousin."

"Thank you for finding me," he said looking at me, then turned his attention to Nikki. "Where is Alex? I figured he'd be here by now."

Nikki's eyes glazed over. Luke slid an arm around her.

"I'm sorry, Jordan," Luke said. "Alex passed away."

Jordan dropped the red Jello on the white sheets. "What? How? Why?"

"He had drugs in his system when he took his snowmobile out for a late-night ride. He crashed." Luke sounded more like a cop than ever with how he described it.

The room was silent. Tears fell from Jordan's eyes as he looked out the window. "I can't believe he's dead," Jordan murmured then turned his attention back to us. "That's why you're all wearing black, huh?"

We nodded. Nikki looked down at her shoes.

"Jordan, we need to ask you a couple of questions about that night," Luke said. "If you're not up for it now, we can come back."

"Jordan?" Debbie's voice came from behind us.

Jordan's eyes widened at the sight of her. She pushed past me and wrapped her arms around his neck.

"Alex's dead," he said, his voice still shaky.

"I know. But I'm so glad you're alive." She still held onto him, but he started to push her away.

"But what about—" he started.

"I think it's best we let you rest before you start talking about things you might not remember." Debbie's voice held a hint of a warning.

Luke stepped closer to the bed. Jordan reached up, unclasped her hands from behind his neck, and pulled Debbie's arms away. "I don't need to rest. You monster," he spat. "You did this to me."

Debbie's face faltered only for the slightest moment. "I don't know what you're talking about." Her voice was innocent and abnormally high pitched.

"Yes, you do. You told me you liked me. That you wanted to be with me." Jordan's lip quivered.

"I did. I do," she said. "Alex and I weren't right for each other. But you and I? We're perfect."

"That night you didn't think so," Jordan said.

"The night you spent with Alex?" Debbie asked. "Didn't I see the two of you *drinking* together?"

Jordan opened his mouth as if he might say something else but quickly closed it.

Nikki turned from the window. "We know you drugged him, Jordan." Tears glistened in her eyes. How did she look so perfect after crying? I looked like a tomato every time I shed so much as one tear.

"I didn't mean to hurt him." Jordan looked at Luke. "He was my best friend. I just wanted to get my shot."

"Your shot at quarterback or Debbie?" I asked.

"Both, I guess," he said staring down at his trembling hands.

"But it backfired," I said a bit more gently now. "The drugs you gave him mixed with the alcohol and his state of distress after telling his dad he was going to quit football—yes, he was going to quit—propelled him into an altered state of mind. He visited his secret girlfriend." I glanced over at Debbie who glared back. "And told her he wanted to run away with her. When she turned him down, he left and took the snowmobile."

I took a breath. "Would you like me to continue?"

Luke raised his eyebrows and smiled.

"As far as what happened to you," I said to Jordan. "Stop me if I get it wrong."

Tears fell from Jordan's eyes.

"When Alex broke up with you, Debbie, you were mad. So mad you decided to seduce his friend."

Neither of them disputed this.

"Jordan, you were drunk. Debbie, you may or may not have been, it's not important." I waved my hand as if batting the idea away. "But you took him back to the reservoir where the three of you had been earlier that evening. I'm guessing you hopped over the gate and walked, probably laughing and holding hands or something stupid like that."

Debbie glared but not an inch of her moved.

"Now, I'm not sure why you did it. Maybe you wanted to get Alex back, maybe you found out Jordan drugged Alex, or maybe you just hated Jordan. But you got him to take off his clothes."

Jordan nodded.

"And then you hit him with your bag," I pointed to the sparkly purse she held in the crook of her arm. The one with a bejeweled star pattern. "And you must have hit him hard because he fell to the ground unconscious."

Luke looked back and forth between Debbie and Jordan, probably trying to figure out if my story was true.

I took a breath. "Then, instead of calling the police, or

an ambulance, you gathered up all of his things and left him there to die."

"You can't prove anything," Debbie said.

"I bet his clothes are still in your car, or maybe your bedroom. And that pattern on your bag matches the exact bruising pattern on Jordan's face."

"And I was there," Jordan finally said. "More or less, that's exactly what happened."

Luke moved toward Debbie and pulled handcuffs from the pocket of his slacks.

Did he carry them with him everywhere?

"Debbie, you're under arrest." He held the handcuffs out. "Do I need to cuff you? Or will you go willingly?"

Debbie looked toward the door where several of her classmates, teachers, and Jordan's parents stood gaping. They must have heard everything we'd said.

"I'll go willingly," Debbie said bowing her head in defeat.

Luke began explaining her rights.

"Do you think I'll be in trouble too?" Jordan asked. His mom had come in to stand by his bedside.

"Why would you be in trouble?" she asked. "It was all that girl's fault you ended up this way."

"He killed Alex." Nikki's voice was hoarse.

"I didn't mean for him to die," Jordan said.

"We'll have to leave that up to the police," I said trying to be as sympathetic as I could. "But I would guess you'd be in some sort of trouble, yes."

Jordan's mom stared at him, "He didn't kill Alex. I did."

Luke stopped talking and stared at her. "I'm sorry, what did you say?"

"I killed Alex." She sank into the chair next to the bed. "I went into his room that night. I just wanted to talk to him—to tell him what he'd done to you," she said to Jordan. "He got worked up and started coding or whatever." Tears streamed down her face. "I thought you were going to die. I didn't realize he was so fragile. He was talking and—"

Nikki looked like she was going to wrap her hands around this woman's neck.

"I think we should go now." I grabbed Nikki's arm and pulled her toward the door.

"She killed him," Nikki said when we'd gotten down to the hospital lobby. I had texted Garrett to see if he could pick us up and take us to our cars.

Alex's heart probably hadn't been up to snuff. Sure she had upset him, but I didn't think she killed him. I couldn't, however, tell Nikki this.

"It's pretty messed up, if you ask me," I said.

"Do you think Debbie really wanted Jordan dead?"

I shrugged. "I don't know. It looks like it. But that's not up to me to find out."

"My uncle was right," Nikki said. "You'd make a good cop."

"I don't want to be a cop. I'm perfectly happy being a park pig," I said, and she actually cracked a smile. "I just wish we could have saved Alex." My emotions crashed over me like a wave. Apparently, now that the mystery was solved, my body thought it was okay to go all weepy-mode on me. Tomato-face was about to come out in full force.

"Me too," Nikki said putting an arm around my shoulders.

We cried together until Garrett showed up.

26

The holiday party and gift exchange made working on Christmas Eve almost tolerable. So did the fact that Shayla and I had met with Marlene the day before and now all I could think of was moving into our gorgeous new apartment.

Life had settled since we were no longer investigating anything. Reginald walked up to my truck carrying an entire tray of brownies.

"These are for you," he said. "For saving Polly."

"I'm so glad she's okay."

"Better than okay. I think the near-death experience encouraged her to live a fuller life."

I searched for hints of a joke in his voice but could find none. "Do you mind if I share these with the other rangers?"

"Not at all," he said. "I heard you figured out what happened with those boys. It was a girl, wasn't it?"

"You were right," I said. "It was a girl."

"Boys and their—"

"Nope." I shook my head. "Don't say it."

He laughed. "Anyone catching anything today?"

The weather had warmed significantly, and fishermen dotted the ice. "Not that I've heard of."

"That's okay. A bad day of fishing is better than a good day at work." He waved as he walked away. "Merry Christmas."

"Merry Christmas," I replied.

"Brownies? I didn't know you baked," Dusty joked when I walked into the banquet hall.

"I don't," I laughed. "Reginald wanted to thank me for saving his dog."

"I helped," Antonio said.

"Don't worry, I'll share." I smiled, but he didn't smile back.

"The brownies or the glory?" Seamus asked.

"Both, I guess." I stuck out my tongue at him.

The banquet hall was completely decked out with lights and tinsel. It was warm and cozy and the perfect place to hold a party.

"Should we start the gift exchange?" Carmen asked, her tone even more bubbly than usual.

Everyone sat in a circle of chairs around a pile of gifts. We'd brought them in on the sly so no one knew exactly which one was from whom. I had my eye on the tiny one on top.

We picked numbers. Greg got number one meaning he got to go first and last. I got five. Right in the middle.

Nikki sat right next to me. "Debbie confessed," she whispered as Greg began looking through the stack of gifts. "But Jordan wasn't as innocent as he acted."

"What happened?" I asked.

"You were right about them coming out here together. They were making out, taking off their clothes, and then Debbie changed her mind, but Jordan didn't want to lose his opportunity. When he wasn't taking no for an answer, Debbie nailed him with her purse, took his clothes, and left. She thought he'd wake up and do the walk of shame. When he didn't show up at morning practice, she called the ranger line."

"She was the hang-up?" I asked.

Nikki nodded. "But she chickened out. Didn't want to get in trouble."

"Well, that backfired. What are they going to charge her with?" I asked.

"Still trying to figure that out. It's a mess."

Greg shook one of the boxes.

"Which one are you going to pick?" Nikki asked.

"Oh yeah, like I'd tell you," I said. She had number four, and even though we were friendly now, I could see her taking it just because I wanted it.

"I want the little one on top," she whispered.

At first, I was irritated, but then I realized I would get to see what it was. And if it was something good, I could steal it.

"I bet it's a ring," she said.

Greg made his first choice and ended up with a collection of coffees. Dusty was next.

"A ring?" I laughed. "Who would bring a ring for a gift exchange?"

She shrugged. "A girl can hope."

"I'm going to get that big one over there," Seamus said from my other side. "The one with the moose wrapping paper that looks like a toddler wrapped it."

That was the gift I'd brought.

And wrapped.

I couldn't bake or wrap gifts. So what?

He'd like the assortment of gift cards I'd wrapped in a big box to throw everyone off. I hardly ever used gift cards and they accumulated at the bottom of my purse. It was a cheap and easy gift idea.

Dusty got a set of grilling tools. "I knew I should have stolen the coffee," he said.

"Don't like grilling?" Seamus asked.

"I already have a set," Dusty replied. "I'm the grill master."

"Prove it," Ben said. "We should have a grill off and see who wins."

"Then they can hold the title of grill master," Seamus agreed.

Dusty sat, his legs spread wide, his arm resting over the back of the chair. "You're on."

"Who has number three?" Carmen asked.

Antonio raised his hand. He took his time circling the pile that was now two presents short. Finally, he pulled one from the inside. "This one looks like it has my name on it," he said. His gaze flickered to me but quickly away. I would have thought saving the dog together might have broken our tension, but for some reason, he was still giving me the cold shoulder.

He carefully unwrapped the bow topping the green and white polka dot paper. When he took the lid off the box, he smiled. "I do not know what I am going to do with these," he said holding up a pair of pink fuzzy dice.

Everyone laughed. He twirled them around and put them back in the box. "If anyone would like to steal some premium fuzzy dice, they are here for the taking."

Nikki stood before Carmen even called her number and snatched the small box off the top of the pile. She ripped the wrapping paper off and pulled out a Denver Bronco's necklace. Someone had to have broken the spending limit, even if the diamonds were fake.

"I guess there's not much chance I'm going to get to keep that, is there?" she asked me.

I handed Carmen my number five and held out a hand. "I'd like to steal that please."

The guys all let out oohs in unison.

Nikki handed me the box. "That's okay, it wouldn't have gone with anything I own anyway."

She stood and grabbed the huge box I'd brought. "Gift cards? Seriously?" She plopped back down in her chair, obviously not thrilled with her gift.

"I'll take those," Seamus said handing his number six to Carmen and taking the box away from Nikki.

"Oh thank God." She stood and weighed her options in the pile. She eyed the necklace I'd just stolen from her. Technically she could steal it back, but she'd made such a fuss about it not matching anything she owned. She turned back and grabbed a small bag.

"I can handle this," she said pulling out a black knit beanie.

It was like a sigh of relief washed through the room. When Nikki wasn't happy, no one was happy.

I glanced up from my necklace to find Antonio staring at me from across the room. I smiled again, but he instantly looked away.

And I had to close the reservoir with him.

Lovely.

Only a few more hours and I'd be home with my family and Garrett and Fizzy opening our one gift.

The gift exchange went quickly after that. Nikki got a few other gifts stolen, but ended up stealing her beanie back in the end. Greg said he was happy with his coffee and the game came to a close.

I fastened the necklace around my neck and tucked it under my uniform. Who might have gotten it? I searched the room. Probably Ben. He was always thinking of how to include Nikki and me. I could see him asking his wife to pick out something she thought we'd like.

Once the party was over, Antonio made himself scarce the rest of the shift, only calling me once to let me know he was taking his dinner break. I had half a mind to confront him about his behavior, but I didn't have the energy.

I was counting down the seconds until the shift was over. The thought of Garrett hanging out with my family without me made me slightly uneasy. I mean, he could hold his own, but I could just imagine my mother pulling out the baby books and telling him stories of how I pooped in the bathtub or something.

I reached into my bag for a snack, and my hand came into contact with something I definitely hadn't put there. I flipped on the truck light and pulled out a worn composition notebook titled *Volume 21*. Nothing else.

The cover made a cracking noise when I opened it to find a loose piece of paper—a letter.

Newbie,

Here you are, a Prairie City Park Ranger. Dream job or not, we can all use a little help. Sometimes the job is fun, sometimes it's not. Sometimes we have good interactions, sometimes they're horrible.

Do as you wish with your time, but don't keep the journal longer than a week. DO NOT sign your name. Anonymity is key. If the journal is lost, it never existed. Start a new one with the sequential volume number.

Once you're finished with it, pass it to another ranger without them knowing it came from you. Put it in their bag, on their desk, in their truck, etc. Never discuss the journal. If someone brings it up, act as if it doesn't exist.

Because it doesn't.

Burn this letter once you've memorized the rules.

Congratulations on being part of the team.

My heart raced. A secret journal? I flipped through the

pages eager to read every last thing within. Some pages held bullet-pointed lists, others poorly drawn comic strips. A few had what looked like songs or poems.

Thoughts and opinions from my co-workers were displayed in all their glory. I couldn't wait to add my own touches.

I gently returned the journal to my duty bag and started around the reservoir to close the back gates. Being part of a team again made me all warm and fuzzy inside.

Once all the gates were closed, I traded my ranger truck for Cherry Anne and made my way to the main gate.

"There are four cars left in the park," Antonio said without looking at me. "I am going to take the truck to the shop."

He pulled away before I could agree.

Three cars had exited the reservoir by the time Antonio pulled up behind me with his CTS-V. The air was warmer than it had been and big fluffy snowflakes fell all around us.

I looked at my watch. Five more minutes and this guy was getting a ticket. It was Christmas Eve for crying out loud.

"Any plans for Christmas?" I asked Antonio.

"I am going to my mother and father's for Christmas dinner."

"That sounds fun," I said.

He grunted.

"Okay, what did I do? Why are you so mad at me?" I was tired of this. "We have to work together, and it's no fun when you completely avoid me all the time."

"Work is not supposed to be fun. It is work."

"It used to be fun. Like when you taught me how to drive the boat."

"You taught yourself. I was only there to help you get out of your head." I thought I saw a faint smile on his lips for a second before it disappeared.

"But it was fun. And now you can't even look me in the eye. Why?"

He took a step toward me. "Do you want to know? Do you really want to know?"

"Yes," I said as bravely as I could with him standing so close to me.

"I cannot stand to be around you. It makes my skin crawl."

Ouch.

I hadn't quite expected that. I looked down at my feet, but he hooked a finger under my chin bringing my gaze back to his.

"Do not take that the wrong way." His Italian accent was strong with emotion. "It is a good and terrible thing. You are so beautiful and funny and you drive me absolutely crazy."

"Okay . . ."

"You do not get it." He dropped his hand back to his side. "You are taken. And I am your co-worker. And we might work together for a very long time. Work romances never work—even if you were single."

"So you're just going to ignore me? We can't be friends?" Tears pooled in my eyes for reasons I couldn't quite put my finger on.

"No. We cannot be friends."

"You're friends with Nikki."

"I do not like Nikki. Not like that."

"You used to," I shot back.

"No." He shook his head. "I did not. There is something about you, Rylie Cooper. Something that makes me want to—" He took a step away and reached both of his hands over his head like he was stretching for a race.

"Want to what?"

"Nothing. It is nothing."

"You have a girlfriend."

"She is not my girlfriend. The Italian Stallion cannot be tamed."

I rolled my eyes. The Italian Stallion crap was getting old. How I'd found it endearing in the first place was beyond me.

"Fine. Then I guess we'll just ignore each other for the next twenty or thirty years until one of us retires or dies." I shook my head. "Do you want to go in and write this guy a ticket or should I?"

I was done waiting. I wanted to get home and drink some eggnog and eat some poorly decorated cookies my nephews had made.

"It is Christmas Eve. Give the guy a break," Antonio said. "And I do not want to ignore each other. I do not know how to behave around you. I say idiotic things, things that could get me slapped or even fired."

"Then don't say those things," I said. "When we were on the boat you didn't say anything bad. Why can't we—"

But before I could finish my sentence Antonio's lips were on mine. His stubble scratched my cheeks as his tongue darted in and out of my mouth.

When he pulled away my lips tingled. The faint scent of his spicy cologne lingered around me.

"Dammit," he said. "I have promised myself I would not do that."

I stood there in shock. I hadn't pushed him away. Why hadn't I pushed him away?

"I apologize," Antonio said. "I will not let it happen again."

"It, uh—" I couldn't find the words. "I have a boyfriend."

"I know." Antonio shook his head.

My fingers touched my lips where he'd kissed me.

Headlights appeared over the hill. The final car zoomed past us.

Antonio closed the gate and locked it in place. "I hope you have a wonderful Christmas, Rylie. I am glad you like the necklace I bought."

"You bought the necklace?" I reached up and touched the metal.

"For you." He shook his head and slid into his front seat leaving me standing in the falling snow with tears in my eyes and a stupid smile on my face.

What had I done?

27

Shayla wasn't answering her phone, and I didn't know who else I could tell. Nikki surely wasn't the right person.

My mind raced back to that kiss. Guilt and pleasure co-mingled in my gut.

How could I have done that to Garrett? I was a cheater. I was no better than my ex-boyfriend Troy and giraffe-girl sidepiece. I had never cheated before.

But Antonio had kissed *me*. Out of the blue. He liked me. And for some reason I wanted him to. Maybe more than Garrett. But why? For the excitement? Because Antonio was the bad boy?

Garrett was the better option. He was the *right* option. Antonio was the typical guy I dated. He would break my heart. And we were co-workers. We couldn't be together. Not openly anyway.

My mind raced. I picked up the phone and dialed the only number I still had memorized by heart that wasn't one of my family members'.

"Hey Rylie," Luke answered on the second ring. I could hear a party in the background.

"Antonio kissed me," I blurted out.

"Merry Christmas to you too." Luke laughed.

"What should I do?"

"Uh, well," Luke hesitated.

I shouldn't have called him. Why had I called him?

"Never mind. I'm sorry. I shouldn't have called you." I pulled the phone away from my ear and moved to hit the end button, but Luke's voice came from the phone.

"Rylie, don't hang up."

I put the phone back up to my ear. "What?"

"Antonio kissed you. Did you kiss him back?" His voice was quiet, and the background noise had silenced.

"I didn't *not* kiss him back."

Luke laughed again. He'd probably already had several drinks. "And you're worried Garrett will be angry with you?"

Is that what I was worried about?

That's what I should have been worried about.

"Uh, yes."

"Just tell him the truth. That Antonio kissed you, that it didn't mean anything, and that you still, uh, love him." Luke choked out the last two words.

"But what if it—"

"Rylie." Luke cut me off. "Antonio is not a guy you want to date. You work together. Plus, he's a player just like Troy. Nikki's told me stories that would make your jaw drop."

I nodded stupidly knowing he was right.

"Garrett is a good guy. The kind of guy you need.

Someone strong and steady and capable of balancing you out. Someone who loves you unconditionally, even if you kiss other guys, or run away and not call him for years at a time."

"Uh, okay," I said.

"He's just a good guy. And you need a good guy. Troy was a tool. Antonio is a tool. Guys like Garrett and me are few and far between, you know?"

"Who are you talking to?" Nikki's voice was in my ear.

"No one," Luke replied, and then the line went silent.

He hung up on me.

I shook my head. Hopefully, Nikki didn't get mad that he was talking to me.

I pulled into my parents' driveway and parked my car next to Garrett's. After a few deep breaths, I was ready to come clean.

28

"Auntie!" Four little boys decked out in holiday pajamas wrapped their arms around me when I walked into what felt like the North Pole. Christmas lights hung all over the enormous living room. A huge tree stood as the focal point near the fireplace, and the kitchen was covered with flour, icing, and sheets and sheets of cookies.

"The place looks amazing Mom," I said. It had been a long time since I'd been home.

"Thank you. Your dad helped, of course." Mom emerged from the dining room wearing a Christmas apron over a green skirt that hit right below the knee and a silky cream blouse. She perched on the arm of Dad's chair, and he put his hand on her crossed legs.

"Well, it's beautiful. You both did a wonderful job," I said.

Garrett walked over, his clothes dusted with flour and his fingers stained from icing. "How was work?" He kissed me on the cheek.

I had been so certain I'd walk in and tell him immediately about Antonio and the kiss, but the look in his eye was of pure Christmas joy. How could I take that away from him?

"It was fine," I said. "Boring really."

"We made you a cookie!" My oldest nephew grabbed my hand and pulled me into the kitchen.

A cookie in the shape of a gingerbread man was completely covered in pink frosting and glittery pink sprinkles.

"It's you," he said waiting for my reaction.

"It's beautiful." I bent down and hugged him. "Thank you so much."

He squeezed me back, and I felt a little bit better.

"Shall we eat?" Mom asked.

"I'm starving," Tom, my brother-in-law, said and wasn't shy about piling his plate high with food the moment he sat at the table.

"You didn't have to wait for me to eat," I said sitting down in the chair Garrett had pulled out for me.

"Of course we did," Dad said with a smile.

"Did you want to change before you eat?" Mom looked at my blue uniform pants and blue t-shirt I wore beneath my button-down uniform shirt.

"No, I'm good." I laughed. "Unless you want me to change."

She glanced at Garrett almost as if she was looking for his answer. He just shrugged.

"I guess you're okay," she said.

"What was that about?" I whispered to him when I sat down next to Garrett at the table.

"What was what about?" he gave me a sly smile. "Stuffing?" He held up a spoonful of my mom's home-made mashed potatoes.

"Mmmm, yes please!" I lifted my plate.

"So you caught another murderer, huh?" Tom asked me from across the table.

The news had been making a bigger deal out of Debbie's arrest than was necessary or true.

"She didn't murder anyone," I replied. "It was a make-out session gone wrong."

"It sounds like she's going to be in a heap of trouble," Mom said. "It's too bad your friend's cousin died."

"Nikki?" Garrett laughed. "Friends huh?"

His tone annoyed me. "She's different than you'd think. Once you get to know her."

"That's my girl. Always seeing the best in people," my dad said beaming.

We finished dinner with minimal talking and maximum eating. Once we were sufficiently stuffed, we headed back to the living room where the boys were prac-tically falling all over themselves to open their one present.

"Okay, but once we're done we have to go to bed so Santa will come," Megan said.

"Santa's not r—" the oldest started but Tom covered his mouth.

"Ready to come yet," Tom said reassuring the other boys.

I glanced at Garrett who was giving me goo-goo eyes. Was he imagining us with kids? My heart raced. Kids? I hadn't even considered kids.

The boys began tearing into their presents—wrapping paper and bows flying everywhere—Megan videoing the entire thing with her phone camera.

I handed Mom an envelope. "This is a little something from Megan and me."

Megan smiled but didn't take her eyes off her boys.

Mom gently pulled the flap up and slid the piece of paper out from within. Tears filled her eyes as she read. "A girls' weekend? Just the three of us?"

"We'll go snowboarding and get massages and sit in the hot springs," I said.

"This had to have cost you a fortune," Mom said.

"Well, since Marlene gave Shayla and me a fantastic deal on an apartment, I had a bit of money left over from what I'd saved."

Her face drooped when I mentioned moving out.

"I wanted to make sure the three of us got to spend some quality time together before I'm gone. Even though I'll only be twenty minutes away."

She smiled. "That's so thoughtful of you. I can't wait." She returned the piece of paper to the envelope and turned to me. "Okay, it's Rylie's turn." Her voice was loud enough to stop my nephews' shouting. She handed me a small square gift wrapped in glossy red paper topped with a silver bow. Maybe it was another necklace.

"Thanks, Mom."

I unwrapped it carefully to find a velvet jewelry box. Hopefully, it wasn't the same necklace. Or maybe she was giving me grandma's pearl earrings. I opened the box and nearly dropped it when I saw the biggest diamond ring I'd ever seen in real life.

"What is this?" I looked around to find Garrett kneeling next to me.

I couldn't breathe.

This couldn't be happening.

Megan was still filming. Mom and Dad were smiling from ear to ear. Even the boys had stopped throwing wrapping paper balls at each other to see what happened.

Garrett's deep blue eyes glistened with expectation.

Hope.

He was talking about love and a future, but all I could think about was earlier that night.

The kiss.

"Rylie Beth Cooper—"

Hearing my full name—something I only heard when my mom was furious with me—pulled my mind back to the moment.

"I know we've only been dating a few months, but I guess when you know, you know."

I had to tell him.

He couldn't do this without knowing the whole truth.

"Will you ma—"

"I kissed Antonio."

The room went silent. Megan dropped her phone.

Garrett stood. "Excuse me," he said before walking out the door.

The ring box was heavy in my hand.

Almost as heavy as the looks on my family's faces.

Shock. Disappointment. Disgust.

What had I done?

Thank you so much for reading *Throttled*. Rylie's really gotten herself into a predicament this time.

If you want to read posts from *Volume 21* of the *Ranger Journal* that was passed along to Rylie, check out my Patreon page (www.patreon.com/stellabixby)! In addition to the journal entries, I will be sharing exclusive content, sneak peeks, and much more.

If you would like a FREE short story about Rylie's first Ice Rescue Training with the Big Mountain Fire Department, go to https://dl. bookfunnel.com/w0b5znx4k1.

And as always, I would be honored and eternally grateful if you would post a review on Amazon and/or Goodreads about the book.

Keep in touch. You can email me at stellabixbyauthor@gmail.com.

XOXO,

Stella Bixby

ACKNOWLEDGMENTS

I have so many amazing people to thank for helping me with this book. As always, God is first and foremost. Every bit of my ability, talent, and determination comes from Him.

My family is my world. Thank you for standing by me as I continue on this crazy writing journey.

Early readers are the absolute backbone of my work. They help me fix things I would never find myself. Dad, Mom, Lurea (Mom), Shawna, Matthew, Lisa, and everyone from the Muddy River Writers and Write On, I cannot thank you enough.

Debbie and Michelle, thank you for your support! I hope you enjoyed the parts you played in this story!

And for all the fans, everyone who reads this book, and

everyone who has read *Catfished* and/or *Suckered*. Thank you, thank you, thank you. I can't wait to share the next one with you!

ABOUT THE AUTHOR

Stella Bixby is a native Coloradan who loves to snow-board, pluck at the guitar, and play board games with her family. She was once a volunteer firefighter and a park ranger, but now spends most of her time making up stories and trying to figure out what to cook for dinner.

Connect with Stella on Facebook, Twitter, and Instagram @StellaBixby.

Stella loves to hear from her readers!
www.stellabixby.com

PATREON DESCRIPTION

About Me:

I never thought I'd be a writer.

I've always been an avid reader, but in high school I was a math and science nerd. I initially went to college for Mechanical Engineering.

Then life happened.

I changed majors a handful of times. I had two kids, got married, got divorced, graduated college, got married again, moved across the country, had another baby, and somewhere in the mix, I decided to write a book.

Enter NaNoWriMo.

In 30 days 50,000 words fell from my brain onto a computer screen.

I was proud. So proud.

Family and friends told me it was good.

I was excited.

But it wasn't good. It wasn't good at all.

Experienced writers murdered it with red ink. (Thankfully they had chocolate to lighten the blow.)

I was deflated but not defeated.

Stephen King's *On Writing*, Anne Lamott's *Bird by Bird*, and Janet Evanovich's *How I Write* were instrumental in my growth. As was writing and writing and writing. And reading and reading and reading. And all of my amazing writing friends along the way.

Nine years after my first NaNoWriMo, I published *Catfished* and haven't stopped since.

Why Patreon?

In the third book of the Rylie Cooper Mystery Series, *Throttled*, Rylie is given a traveling ranger journal. This journal is anonymous and contains entries from all of the rangers.

I almost took it out in my final edits. It didn't have much

of a place for it in the books. But it was too near and dear to my heart.

Enter Patreon.

I'd been toying with the idea of starting a Patreon page, but I wanted to make sure I had content worth paying for. And I think the journal is a perfect starting point!

In addition to the journal, I'm going to be offering other tiers that include exclusive content, a private Facebook group, and early access to books.

Check out the different Tiers starting at $2 per month up at www.patreon.com/stellabixby.

Not sure or have questions? Email me at stellabixbyauthor@gmail.com.

XOXO,

Stella Bixby

www.ingramcontent.com/pod-product-compliance
Lightning Source LLC
Chambersburg PA
CBHW021014120726
47905CB00009B/3000